Cinder Reign
The Enchanted Elixir

Vinn Winters

Finding Heart Publishing

This book is a work of fiction. Names, characters, places, and incidents either are the product of the author's imagination or are used fictitiously, and any resemblance to actual persons, living or dead, businesses, locales or events is entirely coincidental.

www.vinnwinters.com

ISBN 978-1-955282-01-7

Printed in the United States of America

Ancantion

The Third Realm

Acknowledgements

To those who helped me along the way: Though I've thanked you in person, I want to thank you again here. I wouldn't be where I am without your valuable and cherished help. Thank you so very much!

To every reader who craves adventure: This story is for you.

Contents

Cinder Reign

The Enchanted Elixir

Vinn Winters

Prologue

Oh Holy Willow, please see us through this night safely.

"This was a foolish idea; we should have waited until dawn to travel," Edren said, tightening the cloak around himself. The torch-lit caravan creaked through the moonless night. He reached back to touch the crossbow over his shoulder. It was still there, the light weight of it a comfort. People thought he was paranoid because he always kept it loaded, but one could never be too careful traveling on the road.

"I agree. I heard goblins attack at night in these lands," Aline, a half-elf with large blue eyes and fair skin, and the youngest among their group, added. She glanced back and forth into the darkness, while nervously running a hand through her long blonde hair.

"Nonsense, even if the goblin tales were true, they wouldn't *dare* attack our caravan; and if they are foolish enough to try, I'll personally make them wish they'd never left the holes they crawled out of," Bronn, his brick-house of a trading-partner replied. Bronn spoke his mind, often too frequently; but he had the brute strength to enforce it, so Edren tried not to cross him when he would say his piece. A former warrior and bounty-hunter, Bronn always joked about having Orc-blood in his veins.

"Horses don't seem spooked," Tiven exclaimed from the front of the caravan. Tiven was the oldest of the group, with braided, silver hair down to her hips. She frequently exploited those extra years to drive the wagon instead of walking alongside it with the rest of them.

"This *would* be an ideal night for a raid," Edren explained. "We don't even have the cover of moonlight protecting us."

"Well, I heard the goblins were all killed in some big battle a while back," Bronn interrupted, scratching his broad chin. "The king of these lands is said to be some sort of master magician, or a demigod or somethin'. It's said he sent the invading goblin horde runnin' for the hills, killing the goblin leaders by drowning them in a sea of fire. I can't recall the name though; it had something to do with flame... *aarrrgh*! It's on the tip of my tongue..."

"The Battle of Catching Flame?" Edren suggested.

"No, the word 'flame' wasn't in it. I'm sure of that," Bronn corrected.

"A Battle of Ice and Fire?" Aline added.

"Too popular, I think that's the name of every third battle fought across the land. It's something more unique," Bronn said, shaking his head.

"The Battle of Cinder Reign!" Tiven shouted from the wagon.

"That's the most ridiculous one I've heard yet! Everyone knows that cinders cannot rule," Bronn countered.

"Good point," Aline agreed.

"I was just speaking my mind," Tiven huffed.

Edren thought he heard a sound in the distance, but it vanished when he tried to focus on it.

"Anyways," Bronn continued, "whatever the name of that battle was; I heard the only dangerous place in these lands is The Fallen Mountains to the north and some twisted woodland known as The Scarred Forest. Now, do you see any mountains or trees nearby?"

Edren looked around. As far as the torch light carried, all he could see was flat fields.

"No," Edren replied reluctantly.

"If the grass was any higher it'd be a prairie," Tiven added.

"Exactly," Bronn replied, holding his head high. "So unless you're afraid of being attacked by livestock, we've got nothing to worry about."

"Let's just keep moving, I'll feel safer once we've reached the gates of Beckonthrone," Aline added.

"You'll feel safer once you've seen the fortune we'll make in the city marketplace," Bronn said haughtily. "Our wares will get more attention than a newly-opened tavern, and I still have that small box of mermaid scales, which on the Umbra-market should fetch twenty-times our daytime profits."

"Or get an assassin following our tracks," Aline added.

There's that noise again, but where is it coming from? Edren thought as he tilted his head.

"You know what goblins and assassins have in common, Aline? They both fall to my axe," Bronn said with a chuckle.

"It sounds like that axe can slay everything but your ego," Aline muttered loudly.

"What do you mean by that?" Bronn asked.

Tiven laughed.

What is *that sound?* Edren thought, focusing on the faint noise. *It sounds like a flapping of wings, an owl perhaps? Then why is it growing louder…?*

"I'll have you know that it's not the axe that brings the victory," Bronn said stubbornly, "but the one who wields it—"

"Wait, listen!" Edren interrupted. "Do you hear that?"

"The only thing I hear is the shaking of your legs, Edren," Bronn said, turning to him with a furrowed brow. "You have nothing to fear though, if your rattling attracts a curious goblin, I will slay it for you."

"No, I hear it too," Aline said, her eyes shifting to the darkness above them as she drew her bow.

"Sometimes, I am amazed you two are not wed, you have so much in common. You're both terrified of everything," Bronn said while shaking his head. "Without my leadership, our trade would fall apart to nothing but—"

Bronn fell silent as the sound grew even louder, and slowly drew his axe. Edren and Aline anxiously looked towards him, and then at each other.

"What is it?" Edren whispered. "A large crow? An owl? A — a harpy?"

The horses whinnied and reared up.

"The horses are spooked! The horses are spooked!" Tiven shouted.

The noise was no longer a light brush through the air, but a rushing gale that bent the grass around them.

"Maybe it's a storm coming in?" Aline asked, her question sounding like she was begging for it to be true.

"No...," Bronn replied, his eyes widening. "This is no storm."

A powerful gust of wind rushed across the field, blowing out their torches and sending the four travelers sprawling across the ground.

Edren swore as he opened his eyes and looked around. He could see nothing in the total darkness.

The first thing Edren heard was the crashing of the caravan being tipped to its side. The horses squealed, immediately followed by Bronn and Tiven's incoherent shouting.

Edren reflexively reached in his cloak for his crossbow, but it was no longer on him. Cursing, he fumbled around blindly on the ground. Finally he felt the familiar handle of his weapon.

Edren struggled to get to his feet, then froze when he heard Aline's shrill scream.

Swearing again, he raised his crossbow and turned in place.

"Bronn! Aline!" Edren shouted.

The only sound he could hear was the crinkling of his feet against the soft grass and the noise of his own raspy breathing.

"Anyone…" he whispered.

A low rumble made Edren whirl around. He squinted into the darkness.

Where is everyone? he thought. He could feel his heartbeat.

As his sight adjusted, he saw two large midnight eyes, swirling with ruby light, staring back at him.

Beneath the eyes, a giant mouth opened, the jagged teeth becoming more and more visible in the glow of the red light emanating from deep in its throat. The light grew quickly, casting a crimson glow over the grass around him.

With trembling hands, Edren aimed his crossbow and prayed.

Chapter 1

Who else could be out here this late in the evening?

Vyra was sweeping the hay in the stable as she heard approaching footsteps. Her hands gripped the broom nervously when she turned around, only to see Aldrean enter the stables. He was not wearing his regular full-plate armor, the kind she'd seen him in during royal parades, or when he returned to the manor, but was wearing a sharp button-up, black lace shirt, stretched tight against his broad shoulders. A dramatic contrast to his blond hair, but Aldrean could wear anything and look good in it.

"Lord Aldrean!" Vyra curtsied quickly. "What are you doing in the stables at this hour?"

"Oh, my sincerest apologies, milady," Aldrean said, his voice strong and smooth, "I was sneaking out for a midnight ride, I did not think anyone would be out here this late."

Lord Aldrean, despite only being seven years older than she herself, was the Paladin leader of the Silverclad Knights at a mere twenty-five years of age. He had saved the kingdom by leading battles against the goblin onslaught. Not only was he of noble blood, he was a personal favorite of the King, and the closest thing that Beckonthrone had to a celebrity.

"It's no trouble, really," Vyra replied quickly, hoping Aldrean would not sense how anxious she actually was.

"If I may ask, what are you doing out here this late?" Aldrean asked, his green eyes glowing softly in the warm light of the nearby lantern.

"I can leave if you would like." Vyra grabbed the lantern she had brought, and started for the exit, then froze.

You idiot! She thought. *How is he going to mount a horse if you take the only light in the stable?*

"Forgive me, milord," Vyra said as she turned, bringing the lamp to him and holding it out, "you'll probably want this. I can find my way back in the dark—"

"Please," Aldrean said as he grabbed the lamp, his hand softly brushing against hers, "stay."

"You want me to *stay*?" Vyra replied, tucking her copper locks behind her ear.

"Yes, I've noticed you around the manor for quite some time now," Aldrean said.

"It is my duty to tend its upkeep," Vyra said humbly, curtsying once more.

"Indeed, but I still felt a desire to speak with you. You put more effort in than anyone else. You're even out here late at night; when all the other servants are sleeping, here you are, still at it. I admire that about you, Vyra. You put your mind to something, and never quit. You're unstoppable."

He — he knows my name! Vyra's heart jumped in her chest.

"Thank you, that means so much to hear!" Vyra said.

"You have so much potential in you, Vyra. There's a good heart that beats in that chest," Aldrean said with a smile. "I know this may sound unusual but… how would you like to be my first female squire?"

"You mean... I could train to be a knight?" Vyra asked excitedly. Since as far back as she could remember, she had hoped this moment would come.

"Yes, indeed," Aldrean said with a nod. "You have more than earned it. The opportunity is yours, if you want it, of course."

"Yes, milord! Yes!" Vyra yelled, overwhelmed with excitement. Before she could regain her composure, she threw her arms around Aldrean in a tight embrace.

What have I done? Vyra panicked. *Why did I do this? I shouldn't — I shouldn't have done that.*

He smelled the perfect combination of vanilla and cinnamon.

"Vyra..." Aldrean said, sounding surprised.

Vyra did not want to move back, but it felt so good to have his body against hers. She tried to pull away, yet found herself pressing herself against him further. She felt his hands curl around her waist.

"Lord Aldrean, I..." Vyra whispered too close, his breath warming her lips.

"Yes?" Aldrean asked, his eyes never leaving hers.

"I…"

"Vyra! *Vyra!*"

Vyra bolted upward.

Sister Clevora's crow-like shouting woke Vyra from her dream like a bucket of ice water.

Witch's Blight, she thought anxiously, hearing the approaching footsteps, *I fell asleep! I haven't even finished my chores*!

Flustered and blushing, Vyra quickly stood upright and grabbed her broom. She turned away from the stable entrance as she swept, not wanting to see the face that matched Sister Clevora's sigh of frustration.

"Vyra! You were supposed to be finished with this *hours* ago!" Vyra whirled around at the stomp of Sister Clevora's foot. Sister Clevora was a large woman with short, blonde hair; if she had to fight for her life against a bear, Vyra would put her coin against the bear. She would have made a formidable knight herself, if women were allowed to be knights, that is. Beneath her rough exterior, Vyra secretly knew Sister Clevora had a warm heart, even if she never let anyone see it.

For a long time, Vyra had wanted to be a squire. Aldrean had never taken a squire, to her knowledge. She still wanted that… amongst other desires.

"I'm sorry, Sister Clevora! Sunpiercer got out again and I had to chase him through the stable!" Vyra lied. It was a believable lie though; Sunpiercer was the most rebellious of the horses.

"I see, well work twice as hard then," Sister Clevora ordered, still frowning.

"Yes, m'am," Vyra replied.

"I can help," Maek said, following Sister Clevora into the stables. Vyra's eyes met Maek's, and he smiled at her warmly. Maek was a fellow servant; a thin, good-natured young man with short, spiky brown hair. She had known Maek since her childhood; they had been orphans together fighting to survive. Before they were both taken in by Sister Clevora, they were talented pickpockets, so talented they could make a game of hide-and-seek from it. The goal was to start on opposite ends

9

of town, and to see who could find each other first, while picking pockets along the way. If you thought you had more stolen coin, you would try to find the other person before they could steal more; and if not, then avoid the other person until you could steal more. Vyra almost always beat Maek, though whenever he became jealous of her, she smiled and reminded him that they were both winners because now they had all these coins and were never caught.

Though Maek had always adored Vyra, she noticed that he looked at her differently these days, but she could not figure out what had changed.

"See that you do," Sister Clevora replied to Maek sternly, "we're lucky to be the ones responsible for the upkeep of Brightmeadow Manor. Even lowly servant positions like this are rarely given to peasants like us."

Brightmeadow Manor, Vyra thought fondly. Brightmeadow Manor was one of the largest estates in the realm, outside of the royal castle itself. It was the center of command for the Silverclad Knights. It was also Aldrean's home.

"But Sister," Maek said, "didn't we only get these positions because of your connection to the clergy? That you're in service to the High-Priestess Willow?"

"Aye," Sister Clevora said, "and I pulled you two brats up with me. But never forget where we came from, and how quickly we can return to it if we neglect our duties."

"Yes, ma'am," Maek said, picking up a broom to help Vyra.

"Yes, ma'am," Vyra echoed.

"Though," Sister Clevora said, looking as if she was staring off into a distant land that only she could see, "I'd give it all up in an instant to ride that stallion across the kingdom."

Vyra froze in her sweeping, realizing Sister Clevora was not talking about any of the horses in the stable.

"*Sister!*" Maek said, astonished, "you're a woman of the cloth! You should not be thinking such things!"

"*Hush*, child!" Sister Clevora lectured, "I may think how I please. My soul may belong to our beloved God, but my body, Aldrean can do with whatever he pleases."

Maek's jaw looked like it was about to hit the floor. Vyra stifled a laugh.

"We'll have this finished within the hour," she said to Sister Clevora.

"See that you do," Sister Clevora replied, "it needs to be done before—"

The sound of a distant horn jolted her upright.

"The Silverclad Knights have returned early!" Sister Clevora cursed.

"I'll work twice as fast," Vyra said.

"It's too late now. We'll be in more trouble if we aren't at the front of the manor to greet them."

Vyra opened her mouth to protest, but thought better when Sister Clevora grabbed her arm and hastily lead her out.

~

Almost the entire staff of Brightmeadow Manor was present by the time they arrived.

"*Eygodon's piss*, cutting it close, we are," Sister Clevora muttered under her breath.

Vyra barely heard Sister Clevora's swearing, and was glad she was the only one who did. "Eygodon" was a taboo word for one not of noble blood to say in Beckonthrone. Vyra knew the tales by heart. Eygodon was once a warlock of incredible demonic power, leading the vicious goblin hordes known as The Gruharr. Years ago, he joined forces with The Duskpetal Witch, and together they tried to besiege Beckonthrone. King Sargedon defeated the wretched villains, slaying The Duskpetal Witch, and sending Eygodon fleeing back to the shadows. Many still whispered Eygodon's name in private, and he was often the monster in many ghost stories meant to scare children into

11

behaving. However, it was only publicly acceptable for the knights and lords to utter his name, and never in a joking manor.

In the distance, a large band of heavily-armored knights approached on horseback. Each one of them was skilled enough to best at least five of Beckonthrone's soldiers, plus at least two of the royal guard.

Where is he? Where is Lord Aldrean? Vyra thought, squinting at the approaching army, trying to locate the Paladin. *I hope he wasn't hurt.*

"Fear not, beloved peasants! Orbit has arrived!" a small, bulky knight wearing full-plate armor shouted as he led the way. He quickly hopped off his horse, nearly falling face-first into the dirt as he did. Catching himself at the last moment, he turned to face the silent crowd as if nothing had happened.

"I said *Orbit has arrived*! Do you not know who I am? I am *O-o-o-o-orbit the Omnipotent*!" the gnome barked loudly, then pounded his chest plate with his tiny fist.

"We know who you are, you live here!" one of the younger servants yelled from the crowd.

"Then why do you not cheer for Orbit?" Orbit shouted, slamming his giant hammer to the ground, "Orbit has arrived!"

"*Yaaaaaaay,*" the crowd yelled unenthusiastically.

"Hmph," Orbit grunted. "It needs work, but an acceptable start."

While the tiny warrior was the second strongest of the Silverclad Knights; he was also the loudest and the most likely to leave the largest mess for the servants to clean up, which is why he was not very popular among the staff.

"There he is! There's Lord Aldrean!" shouted Jeuvine, a fellow servant and a friend of Vyra.

Vyra eagerly looked back to see Aldrean approaching. Vyra wondered why the leader of the Silverclad Knights was riding at the rear of the army, but then she noticed the little girl sitting just in front of him. She held onto the horse tightly; her body was covered in scrapes and bruises.

"What happened to her?" Amberleen asked, as she ran up to Aldrean's horse. As the Head Housekeeper of Brightmeadow Manor,

Lady Amberleen ensured that all the servants were performing their assigned duties. Lady Amberleen's brown hair was pulled back, revealing a face sculpted to judge remorselessly. Though Amberleen appeared proper and civilized, Vyra thought there was nothing "lady-like" about Amberleen; she found the woman's personality to be as cold as the grave.

"Nothing to worry about," Lord Aldrean said calmly. "We found this little one wandering out in the wild during our trip back. I suspect she's from Solria or Trael, but she hasn't spoken since we found her."

"Well, give her here," Amberleen said, holding her arms up, "we'll see to it that she has a nice meal and bed to rest in until we can figure out where she belongs."

Aldrean reached to gently lift the girl, but she turned and clung to him.

"Hey, hey... it's okay," Aldrean said softly to the girl, "you're safe now. No one is going to hurt you here. These are my friends; you can trust them, okay?"

The girl looked up at him and nodded. He gently lifted her from the horse and into Lady Amberleen's arms.

"Go easy on her; it looked like she had been wandering for a while outside of the city walls before we found her. I don't know where the cuts and bruises came from. Her body was covered in ash when we first found her. We cleaned her up the best we could; if you could see to her wounds too, I would appreciate it."

"Worry not, milord. We will take good care of her," Amberleen said confidently. Looking down at the child, she smiled and added, "First we'll clean your wounds, and then bandage those cuts up. Then we'll get you something nice and warm to eat."

"Thank you, as always your diligence is valuable," Aldrean said with a smile. Amberleen nodded and carried the girl off towards the manor.

"I would like to update you all on the occurrences of the kingdom!" Aldrean shouted as he turned to the staff.

"Lord Aldrean, I mean no disrespect but we are not the King or the war council," a servant yelled, "why are you telling us this?"

"While this is true, I assure you these words will also be spoken to our beloved King and council. You are my people, and each one of you are dear to me," Aldrean said, placing a hand over his heart, "you deserve to know as much as anyone else."

There were cheers from the crowd.

"There he goes, flashing his charm again," Sister Clevora muttered, "he really knows how to get the people to love him."

"You mean, by treating the people with respect and dignity?" Vyra asked.

"Aye," Sister Clevora replied with a nod.

"And that scrumptious body doesn't harm his cause either," she added enthusiastically.

"*Sister*!" Maek hissed from behind them. "You are a woman of the cloth!"

"Only until he takes it off," Sister Clevora said with a smirk.

Maek gasped. Vyra snorted stifling a laugh.

"Another horde of goblins thought they could threaten our beloved kingdom," Aldrean said. "They continue their wild assaults from the north, believing that their legions will soon overwhelm us."

"Are they The Gruharr?" another servant asked.

"We are not sure. There are many goblin tribes infesting our beloved land of Ancantion. With the frequent and strategic attacks, we suspect that it may indeed be The Gruharr, being led by the unscrupulous, goblin-warlock Eygodon," Aldrean said gravely.

There were murmurs of concern from the crowd.

"But fear not," Aldrean added confidently, "we beat those vile creatures back to the caves they crawled out from. If Eygodon is leading them, he is too cowardly to dare show his face against our virtuous strength. While I would highly advise against venturing out of the city; I assure you, within these walls you are safe and protected."

The crowd cheered as Aldrean waved, and then The Silverclad Knights dismounted their horses and continued their march into the manor.

14

"Even though he is of noble class and we are mere servants, he always treats us like equals," Sister Clevora said, her eyes beaming with admiration.

"Do you think we'll always be mere servants?"

"Not you, you'll become a squire one day, like you've always wanted," Sister Clevora said, flashing Vyra a wide smile.

"Even though I'm not a noble, and women can't become squires?" Vyra asked, as the crowd began to disperse.

"Oh, you'll get there," Sister Clevora said, putting her hand on Vyra's shoulder, "you're too damn good to not be, and you're only eighteen years of age. They just need to pull their heads from their arses and see it, that's all."

Vyra smiled wildly.

"Hey, who knows," Sister Clevora said with a shrug, "maybe you'll be the knight who finally puts an end to that wicked Eygodon."

"Shhh!" Vyra said. "Don't say his name out loud."

"Bah! I don't fear words," Sister Clevora huffed.

"Do you think I could ever be Lord Aldrean's squire?" Vyra asked, trying to change the subject.

Sister Clevora sighed. "'Tis a nice dream to have, although Lord Aldrean's never had a squire before. But if it happens, you need to put in a good word for me, promise?"

"Promise," Vyra said with a nod.

Vyra tried to embrace Sister Clevora, but she had already moved towards the footmen holding the horses.

"We need to get these back to the stables, then finish cleaning them," Sister Clevora said, her tone reverting back the order from a supervisor.

"Yes, Sister," Vyra said with a nod.

Chapter 2

Eygodon had just about finished purchasing his list of ingredients, when his keen ears overheard his name mentioned from behind a building. Curious, he slipped into the alleyway to find a tall, short-haired man gossiping with a long-haired woman. Both looked like commoners who aspired to become nobility above all else. They both simultaneously cast him a glare as he approached.

"Did I hear that you have gossip to share?" Eygodon said, briefly flashing his jagged teeth with a flashy smile.

"We didn't say 'nothing!" the man barked. "Beat it!"

"A pity, I might have some to share myself."

Their scowls quickly vanished.

"Well, we always love something new," the woman said, "I am Willa, a seamstress from the infamous Brightmeadow Manor."

"Hail, stranger," the man said, "and I'm Theo, one of the King's most favored farmers from just outside the city walls."

"It is an honor to meet such well-established individuals," Eygodon said smoothly, disregarding their attempts to brag. "I am merely Nodogye, a wandering scholar. But I hear much on my travels."

Eygodon tightened the hood over his head, further covering his ears. He was only half-goblin, and thus was able to blend in with humans with ease. He had a strong jawline, which he preferred to hide beneath a short beard. His only prominent goblin features were his large pointy ears, slightly jagged teeth, and the irises of his eyes being bright amber. He could convincingly pass for an elf if not for his eyes, and if elves more frequently traveled to these outer lands.

Most humans hated goblins because of their presumed tendency to attack everything; which was only partially true. Much like humans, while some goblins chose a path of primal aggression, there were many intelligent and civilized goblins that were able to establish advanced societies, both in technological discoveries and cultural growth. The intelligent goblins also possessed adept critical thinking skills, which made for incredibly poor minions. Thus, years of fostering a society of goblins that preferred aggression, and kindling their savage instincts had been vital to creating the primal swarm that was feared as The Gruharr. Remnants of the horde still aimlessly rampaged through the wilds to this day. Eygodon had done his job, and he believed he had done it rather well.

"Well, have you heard about the goblin raid in Trael? They say the town guard would have been overwhelmed if the Silverclad Knights hadn't been nearby! I heard that even the evil warlock Eygodon might be behind it!" said Theo.

"Actually, I heard he was more of a sorcerer, really," interjected Eygodon. *Why do they always call me a warlock?* he thought, suddenly irritated. The only warlocks in recent Ancantion history were practically necromancers. Sorcerers were graceful and wise, bending the elements of the natural world to their will like a form of art.

"No, I heard it myself from Aldrean at Brightmeadow Manor, he's an unscrupulous warlock," Theo said confidently.

"He said *what*? That flaming piece of centaur shi— wait, do you even know what *unscrupulous* means?" Eygodon asked pointedly.

"I think it means... uh... bad," Theo answered, scratching his head.

"Are you sur-r-r-e?" Eygodon purred.

"I...err..." Theo said, looking like he was about to have a headache.

"Well, do you know what *unify* means?" Eygodon asked.

"Doesn't it mean, to bring — to bring people together?" Willa answered, uncertain.

"It does indeed!" Eygodon replied. "Well, my good sir and miss, a shorter word, *scrupulous*, means diligent and avoidant of wrongdoing. Aldrean merely combined the two words, *unify* and *scrupulous*, making a higher form of the meaning *unscrupulous*; which actually means the pinnacle of ethics and moral virtue."

"Uh, what does pinnacle and virtue mean?" Theo asked.

Eygodon sighed. "It means the best good person around," he said slowly, as if talking to a toddler.

"Oh! Well, that doesn't seem right." Willa tilted her head.

"The paladin said it himself, did he not? Are you questioning the wisdom of our great Lord Aldrean?" Eygodon replied.

"Certainly not!" Willa said.

"We would never dare question the great Aldrean," Theo said, following Willa.

You'd be wiser to doubt that arrogant dragon-rectum, Eygodon thought bitterly.

"Good, then be sure to tell your friends the insight that you have learned here," Eygodon said, with a nod.

"Thank you, No-d-dow-gey," Willa said, still struggling to pronounce his fake name correctly.

"It's Nodogye," Eygodon said.

Eygodon was considering leaving when he caught Theo repeatedly glancing at him, and then over his shoulder.

"Is something wrong?" Eygodon asked.

"Did anyone ever tell you, Nodogye, that you look a lot like the warlock Eygodon?"

"Sorcerer," Eygodon reflexively corrected. Irritated, he whirled around to see the stone wall behind him had a "Wanted" poster with his picture on it. Well, it was a similar variant of him, at least.

Pixie-bottom! They have Wanted posters of me now? Who gazed upon my face long enough to sketch it? Clearly a blind man, because these features are all wrong! My nose and ears are not that large! And a wart on my nose, seriously? *I do not know what is more offensive, that this cartoon of me was created, or that this peasant believes it looks enough like me to compare*!

"Hey, it does kind of look like you," Willa added, "could you be a cousin of his or—"

Eygodon chanted a quick incantation and Theo and Willa vanished, their clothes falling to the brick-floor below. There were small rustles of movements within the garments, and two toads hopped out of the clothes.

"There we go," Eygodon said, picking up the two toads and turning down a darkened alley.

"Fear not, my tiny friends," Eygodon said with a smirk as he walked down the darkened alley, "the spell will wear off in a few hours, yet I wonder if anyone will *actually* believe your tale when they find you naked in High-Priestess Willow's Gardens... if they don't step on you first."

~

"Are you sure we should be taking this route?" Vyra asked.

"If we do not stop, I doubt they will even notice us," Sister Clevora replied.

"These buckets are heavy," Vyra said, breathing heavily.

"I know. But keep quick feet, my dear," Sister Clevora said briskly, "we don't want to get in trouble for lingering in the high gardens."

Outside of the palace gardens, the high gardens of Brightmeadow Manor was one of the most popular places in all of Beckonthrone for nobles to idly wander and promenade. Those of lower class were only permitted for garden maintenance, and only if there were no nobles present. The High-Priestess Willow once declared publicly that the high gardens of Brightmeadow Manor were her favorite place in all of Beckonthrone, giving the gardens the nickname of Willow's Garden.

"Yes, Sister Clevora. I'm right behind you—" Vyra froze when she saw Lord Aldrean approaching the gardens. He was wearing a simple white button-up shirt beneath a long cerulean jacket, embroidered in elegant golden brocade. Several other knights were walking beside him, but parted ways as he entered the high gardens.

He's there, he's right there in front of me! Vyra thought, setting down her buckets as if in a dream, and eagerly walked towards him. The sight of Aldrean completely wiped all thoughts of her current errand from her mind. *What if this is my opportunity to be a knight? He looks to be in a tranquil mood. Maybe if I approach him now he'll let me speak*!

"What sort of *vile intrusion* is this?" A sharp feminine voice jolted Vyra back from her ambitions.

Head Housekeeper Amberleen hissed as she stepped in between Vyra and her goal. Amberleen's dark-brown hair was again pulled back, highlighting the impression of the strict, shrewd woman that she was. She dressed well, not as fancy as nobles, but upscale enough to distinctly separate her from the lower servant-classes.

A young, blonde-haired noble woman in the garden looked over at the conflict. Vyra suspected the cost for the woman's elaborate hair-style and exquisite dress alone was more than she could have stolen in a lifetime of pick pocketing on the streets. When the noble woman's eyes met Vyra's, she crinkled her nose in disgust.

Pretty only on the outside, Vyra thought spitefully.

"Away with you, you've done enough damage for today," Amberleen said, grabbing Vyra by the ear. Vyra winced silently, but held her tongue knowing another outburst here would certainly get her beaten, or worse.

As Amberleen pulled Vyra away, she caught a glimpse of Aldrean approaching the young, noble woman in the garden; he seemed completely unaware of Vyra's crime of breaking into nobles' territory, and the noblewoman seemed blissfully prepared to pretend Vyra had never existed.

"I hope you are enjoying your visit," Aldrean said, his voice as smooth and confident as it was in her dreams.

"Lord Aldrean!" the noble woman gasped with joy, "you grace me with your presence!" "You must be mistaken, to be in the presence of such beauty such as yours, I am the one *truly* graced. I plan on a casual stroll around the manor, would you honor me with your presence?" Aldrean asked, gently grasping the noble woman's hand and giving it a soft kiss.

"I would be delighted, Lord Aldrean," the noble woman said. She blushed with a picturesque smile, but all Vyra could remember was her ugly, scrunched glare.

Then they were out of the gardens, Sister Clevora quickly trailing behind. Amberleen marched her around the manor walls, to a more secluded place free from the eyes of the nobles.

"You are but a mere servant girl!" Amberleen barked, finally releasing Vyra, "you barely have the privilege to talk to someone of my status, and only for reasons related to your duties. Lord Aldrean is far *far* beyond your caste."

"And what if he wishes to talk to me?" Vyra asked defiantly.

Amberleen gasped. "You would dare dream of such an encounter?"

Then Amberleen laughed loudly. "I suppose Lord Aldrean may talk to whomever he wishes, but everyone knows that he only talks to women of high breed."

"You said that he talks to whomever he wishes. So, if he wanted to talk to me—" Vyra protested.

"Remember your place, child," Amberleen said with a scowl, "nobody *wants* to talk to you."

"Please, forgive her," Sister Clevora said, rushing to Vyra's defense, "she was not feeling herself this morning. She will come to her senses, Amberleen, I will see to it personally."

"She better come to them quickly, or it's on you, dear," Amberleen scoffed, making a face of disgust, "and see to it that she stays out of the manor until she is of her right mind. If she is ill, we would not want those of *importance* to succumb to whatever she carries."

Vyra's fists were clenched so tightly she could have sworn she drew blood.

"Remember this lesson, or I will see you back to the gutters you came from so quickly, not even your guardian Sister Clevora will know where you went," Amberleen spat.

"We are sorry," Sister Clevora interjected, subtly elbowing Vyra in the side, "we accept your generous mercy."

"Yes, please forgive me. I was foolish to forget my place," Vyra forced the words out of her mouth, each one feeling like a knife to her chest.

"Yes, you were," Amberleen said, raising her head up with a triumphant smirk, "and you better not forget it. I won't show you pity next time."

"I am... grateful for your patience with me." Vyra was so angry she wanted to cry.

A chorus of screams reached their ears from where they had just left.

"There are nudists in the gardens!" a noble woman yelled.

"How abhorrent, somebody summon the guards!" a noble man shouted.

"And a physician, Lady Berkintar has fainted!" another noble woman added.

"Now off with you. I'm sure there is more work that needs to be done," Amberleen turned and paced briskly back to the gardens.

"Don't you pay that witch any mind," Sister Clevora said under her breath as they walked away, "you play your part so she won't send you away, but you did nothing wrong. Being of 'higher status' don't mean you need to act like you got a lance up your backside."

Vyra laugh softly. Sister Clevora always had a way of cheering her up.

Chapter 3

"**A**ldrean! *Aldrean*!" a loud husky voice penetrated the bedroom.

"Who is that?" Cothreen asked, arching her back and pressing into the sheets.

Aldrean sighed. "No one important," he said. "Maybe if we're quiet, he'll go away." He grimaced at the door.

"Easier for you… than me, milord," Cothreen breathed out, her cheeks a bright rosy pink.

"*Aldrean*!!" The husky voice was so loud through the door that it practically echoed this time.

Aldrean groaned in frustration.

Cothreen gasped softly as Aldrean made one final thrust before he withdrew himself from the blonde-hair noble woman. Putting on a silk robe, he made his way across the luxurious room to the chamber door.

"But I'm not dressed!" Cothreen protested.

"You better find a way to cover up quickly then," Aldrean said indifferently as he continued toward the door.

Cothreen lunged towards the sheets, pulling them up to her chest just as Aldrean opened the door.

"Aldrean! Why are you sulking in your room this day?" Orbit barked. "You missed the commotion in the gardens!"

"I was in the gardens only recently," Aldrean replied.

"Well then, you just missed the talk of the day! Commoners snuck into the high gardens and were running around *unclothed*! The guards were trying to catch them, but of course wearing armor they weren't fast enough to catch them. Orbit would have stepped in to help out, but it was too much fun watching the guards trip and fall over each other as they tried to catch the naked—"

"Is there a reason why you are here?" Aldrean asked, with growing irritation.

"Ah yes," Orbit said, clearing his throat. "King Sargedon demands our presence in the royal throne room for tactical discussion. Some town on the outskirts of Ancantion got attacked by another goblin raid and—*o-o-o-o-o-h*."

The gnome warlord momentarily fell silent as he caught a glimpse behind Aldrean, to the noble woman on the bed.

"Got company again, eh?" Orbit said with a wink, "you know, if Orbit slayed half as many goblins as the women you slay with that sword beneath your belt, Orbit would be the champion of these lands."

"*Silence*, before I meld you and your miniature plate armor into a cannonball," Aldrean hissed, "besides, I have refined taste in only the highest quality of woman."

"Indeed," Orbit replied, stroking his dark beard, "if high quality means anything you can reach from your bedroom. Orbit admires your lethargy!"

"Don't make me step on you," Aldrean snarled.

"That is what the full-plate armor is for," Orbit said with a chuckle, "now Orbit enjoys this battle of words and wit, but the Palace summons us both."

"I gathered that much," Aldrean said flatly.

"And do not fear, Orbit will tell King Sargedon you are arriving from out of the city, give you a little longer to... finish up," Orbit said with a wink.

"Don't bother. I'll be down momentarily," Aldrean growled, "you've already killed the mood."

"*Ah-hah!*" Orbit shouted so loudly that both Aldrean and Cothreen jumped, "yet another death by the hands of Or-r-r-rbit the Omnipotent! These goblins will stand no chance against Orbit's might!"

Aldrean slammed the chamber door. Echoes of Orbit's self-motivating battle cries echoed down the hallway.

"I'm... going to go now," Cothreen said, filling the air with awkward tension.

"Please, see that you do," Aldrean said sternly, and turned towards his bathing chambers.

A curse upon that mule-headed gnome, Aldrean cursed.

~

Aldrean paced briskly down the enormous palace hallways. Large, elaborate stone statues loomed overhead from both sides of the hallway, each remembering a different hero from times past.

Perhaps I should have accepted that obnoxious gnome's offer to buy me additional time, Aldrean thought as he straightened his collar.

"Well, look who *finally* arrived," said De'eyzen, the King's Advisor, as he lazily stroked his beard as Aldrean walked a little more quickly into the throne room.

"My humblest apologies, your Majesty," Aldrean said, ignoring De'eyzen's sneer. He walked by Orbit, noticing the gnome's worried look for him as he passed. Stopping at the base of the stairs that ascended to the throne he quickly bowed; keeping his eyes to the floor, hoping the king would give him permission to raise his head.

"Your tardiness is *not* appreciated," King Sargedon's voice boomed so loudly it echoed.

"Forgive me, my liege. It won't happen again," Aldrean replied humbly, still not daring to look up.

"It better not," De'eyzen spat, standing beside the obsidian throne.

"Your Majesty, Orbit has found another man whom he believes might yield promise in the fight against the goblin hordes. He appears to have the potential of a great knight," Orbit interjected, in a blatant attempt to cheer the King up or at least distract him.

"Very well," King Sargedon replied, "you may bring him in."

"At once, your Majesty," Orbit bowed and quickly spun around towards the guards at the throne room doors.

"By his Majesty's decree, bring in Sir Mondrem, of the Green Cliffs!" De'eyzen shouted, with minimal enthusiasm.

The doors slowly opened. Keeping his head down Aldrean turned to see a huge, brown-haired man approach. He was bulky, and had to be at least eight foot tall. Aldrean suspected that the man was a third-generation descendant of a giant to be that large.

Sir Modrem nodded as he approached Orbit, a smug expression on his face. There were not many knights of giant lineage; he had a significant edge on the competition.

"Sir Modrem of the Green Cliffs, you stand in the grace of our majesty, his Royal Highness, King Sargedon, Sovereign of Ancantion, and Ruler of the Third Realm. Step forward and pledge your eternal fealty," De'eyzen said.

"It is an honor," Sir Modrem said as he stood before the throne. He began to kneel, but then stood back up.

"But where is he?" Sir Modrem asked, looking around.

Aldrean's eyes widened, anxiety swept through him like a tidal wave.

"But *where... is...?*" De'eyzen repeated with frustration growing so quickly that his left eye had begun to twitch.

"Yeah, *where* is he?" Sir Modrem asked again.

"You *stand* before his Greatness, young knight," De'eyzen snarled.

Aldrean frantically looked at Orbit, whose mouth was slowly dropping open.

"You didn't *tell* him?" Aldrean hissed.

"Orbit thought he had! Orbit really did!" Orbit whispered back.

"Will you now pledge your eternal fealty?" De'eyzen repeated.

"Is this a hoax? I'm not pledging my loyalty to some damn tabby cat just because he's sitting in the King's throne," Sir Modrem protested.

There was a thud and clanking of metal, as Aldrean then Orbit fell to the floor in shock.

"*Such impudence!*" De'eyzen screeched.

"Orbit, what have you done?" Aldrean said, finally daring to look up.

"Forgive him, my liege!" Orbit pleaded, "Orbit thought he knew!"

"Impudence? Because I won't bow before a vagrant animal that stole the King's chair?" Sir Modrem argued.

De'eyzen gasped.

"Oh, *divine presence*," Aldrean uttered, the closest a Paladin was allowed to swear in public.

"You idiot!" Orbit yelled at Sir Modrem, "Shut up before—"

"*Silence!*" King Sargedon's voice was so loud that it echoed several times

The room fell silent, all eyes turned to the tiny, striped cat sitting on the throne.

"I *am* indeed King Sargedon," the feline's words were like thunder.

"You? *Impossible*," Sir Modrem said with a laugh, "King Sargedon slayed three trolls with only an iron dagger. He defeated the Dragon of the Windward Coast by strangling it to death with just his bare hands. During the Battle of Cinder Reign, he slayed the vicious Duskpetal Witch and sent the warlock Eygodon and his goblin minions fleeing into the Fallen Mountains. You, you're just a talking cat."

"Please, your Majesty," De'eyzen pleaded, "let me make an example of this hooligan. A lifetime in the dungeon will surely teach him the error of his ways."

"You know your history, lad. I have done everything you said, and more," King Sargedon said, ignoring De'eyzen as he hopped from his throne and climbed down the steps, one paw at a time.

"Defeating the Duskpetal Witch came at a price," the cat continued without blinking, "as we fought back her hordes, the wretched hag prepared a ritual to strike me down. We interrupted the rite before it was complete. In her final acts, she managed to activate the spell prematurely, and though it did not eradicate me as she'd planned, it did reduce me to a, well, smaller form."

Modrem yelped as a thwack from Orbit's hammer to the back of his leg brought him to his hands and knees. The young knight's face was now inches away from Sargedon's fuzzy nose.

"I will grant mercy to you this time, as few have seen me in the years since the battle with the Duskpetal Witch," Sargedon said calmly, staring at Modrem. The cats pupils narrowed to tiny slits, "but cross me again, and I will make sure you're on the front line of every battle against the goblin hordes; and if the knights are faced against The Gruharr, you'll get a head start, and I will ensure that the rest of my army will not quickly follow your charge. Do we have an understanding?"

"Yes, my liege. We do," Modrem said, his voice shaking.

"Good," King Sargedon purred, "now *pledge*."

Sir Modrem was so traumatized by the ordeal that Orbit had to help him walk out of the throne room.

"I'm sorry Orbit, I didn't realize—" Sir Modrem whimpered.

"Shut your trap! You buffoon, Orbit is *extremely* disappointed in you," Orbit whispered sternly.

Aldrean could not help but quietly chuckle at the sight of a short gnome helping the large, shivering man leave, the royal doors quickly shutting behind them. The Paladin turned to face the throne just as King Sargedon leapt gracefully onto it.

"Well," King Sargedon stared down at Aldrean, "though clearly unplanned, Orbit was indeed successful in momentarily distracting my mind from your tardiness."

"He is as graceful as a blind ox, but very loyal and means well," Aldrean said, trying to defend Orbit without further angering King Sargedon.

"I will look past it," Sargedon said, scratching his ear with his foot, "Orbit is a powerful and valuable warrior, like yourself, and occasionally that knowledge gives me enough patience to look past your blunders."

"You honor me with your tolerance, Majesty," Aldrean said gratefully.

"Indeed, but do not take it for granted," Sargedon said with a feline huff. "Unlike your pledge to me, my patience with you is not eternal."

"I understand, Majesty," Aldrean said, "now how may I be of service?"

"The people are uneasy," King Sargedon said solemnly. "The reports of missing people are rising. Many were said to be traveling between Solria and Trael at night, but now there's a similar pattern on the roads between those cities and Beckonthrone. A ravaged caravan was even found on the road south of Beckonthrone; apart from the caravan, there was no sign of a struggle, but the ground was stained with blood."

"That is concerning," Aldrean replied. "What do you think the cause is?"

"Our scouts report that the town of Twin Falls is suffering from nightly goblin raids. Our soldiers fight them off, but the fiends return the next night in greater numbers. Given the town is on the outskirts of our realm, I only have a small bastion positioned there; and I doubt there will be enough to hold them off much longer."

"That is an issue that requires attention," Aldrean said, stroking his chin. "But Twin Falls is near Titan's Pass, at the opposite edge of our realm. Are we sure the raids are connected?"

"You remember what viciousness The Gruharr is capable of, especially if they have an ambitious leader."

"Goblins are such vile creatures," Aldrean spat, "do you believe the Duskpetal Witch to be behind this?"

King Sargedon's legacy had been countless victories for the human empire, greatly aiding in the human expansion through Ancantion. An unexpected by-product of this was the King's belief that the strength of the human empire heavily relied on himself and those close to him appearing invulnerable at all costs. So it was not commonly known to the people of Ancantion that though the Duskpetal Witch's ritual failed in killing King Sargedon, it had given the Duskpetal Witch enough time to escape; the king was nearly killed by the warlock Eygodon, but was saved in the final moment by Aldrean.

Not many soldiers had witnessed the King being turned into a cat, and the ones that had were denounced through the creation of new laws, so no one would ever believe the tale if it was told. It was not a decision that sat well with Aldrean; but King Sargedon did not believe order could be maintained if the people knew their powerful king had been reduced to a common cat. It was not fair or just, but condemning the witnesses to martyrdom was what the King thought necessary to keeping order, so Aldrean held the secret in silence.

"I would suspect so, or a warlord that seeks her alliance," Sargedon said, "they're testing the walls of our realm, looking for a weak point to break in."

"We will not grant them such relief," Aldrean growled. "Just like in the Battle of Cinder Reign, I am your sword, your Majesty. And I will strike down any darkness."

"I know you will," Sargedon said, and then yawned, "take fifty men with you, clear out the area and be back by tomorrow evening."

"Fifty men is more than enough," Aldrean replied with a nod, "Do you think the wicked Eygodon might be behind this as well?"

"Perhaps, but I would not wager upon it," Sargedon said between paw licks. "We lost the Sixth Realm to the united forces of Eygodon and the Duskpetal Witch. I have no doubt that this realm would likely have fallen too had we not been victorious at the Battle of Cinder Reign. Though neither died at that battle, most the goblin attacks since have lost their strategic edge; they are reckless to the point where I wonder if these goblins are even part of The Gruharr or are just forgotten remnants. This leads me to suspect that, if they both are alive, they no longer continue their alliance. But whether Eygodon has broken from the Duskpetal Witch, is fighting elsewhere, or has died, to that I am uncertain."

"I doubt he is dead, at least not until I finish him off," Aldrean said with a snarl, his hand tightly gripping the handle of his sword.

"I understand your animosity towards the warlock. It is akin to my hatred of the Duskpetal Witch," Sargedon said, his tail flicking back and forth. "If he still does yet live, I am confident he will not be so fortunate the next time your paths cross."

"I hope you're right, Majesty," Aldrean said, "I will set out immediately."

"You have my blessing," King Sargedon reached out to the Paladin with one paw, "now go, and rid my lands of this goblin scourge."

Chapter 4

"**Y**ou're doing it wrong again," Vyra whispered playfully to Maek, after seeing him soak the jacket in the wooden tub of heated water.

"What do you mean *I'm doing it wrong*?" Maek argued defensively. "It needs to be washed, does it not?"

The servants had rotating shifts on who was assigned to wash the clothes of the higher classes. Fortunately, they did not need to travel to the public wash-rooms in the city, as Brightmeadow Manor was large enough to have its own wash-room in the basement.

"Maybe if you were washing *our* clothes," Vyra explained, "but noble clothes are only fully washed with soapwort every third time. The other times they are only to be shaken to remove dust, or lightly beaten if necessary."

"She's right, you're very much screwing it up," Jeuvine, a fellow servant, added as she snickered loudly.

"*Witch's Blight*! *Maek Trokinson*!" Sister Clevora yelled as she entered the room, her voice so loud it almost echoed. "By the way that you clean our nobles' clothes, I would presume that you come from a long lineage of ragged highwayman and cutthroats!"

"It's not *that* bad!" Maek said with a sigh.

"It's pretty bad," Jeuvine teased.

"Look. I'm a *man*," Maek protested, "my duty should be to slay the wild beasts of the forest, and bring back the meat for dinner; not to dally cleaning clothes and trading hearsay."

"If I wanted a boar slain for my dinner, I'd choose Vyra in a heartbeat," Sister Clevora countered, "she could probably bring back twice the bounty I request, while you would wind up food for the forest gremlins."

"Sister Clevora, why would you say such an awful—" Maek started, his jaw dropping.

"Sorry, dear, but I've seen Vyra practice. She is unquestionably the best fighter of the lot of us."

"Just doing what I can to prepare for squire-hood, if such a thing is possible for me," Vyra added humbly.

"You know that women cannot become squires," Maek countered, "it's the law."

"It's a foolish law," Sister Clevora spat, "Vyra could best the finest squires in the kingdom, and she's only been alive for eighteen years. She has earned her place as a squire."

"We could spar if you'd like," Vyra said, flashing Maek a smile, "I've two sturdy broomsticks that would make for fine swords—"

"*So*, when do you apply the soapwort again?" Maek asked meekly, desperate to change the subject. Vyra and Maek had sparred many times; not only had Maek never won, but he usually wound up covered in bruises.

"As usual, when it comes to confrontation, you're all huff," Sister Clevora said, she shook her head and laughed.

"How *are* you a Sister?" Maek asked, astonished by Sister Clevora's words.

"My intelligence and wit, of course," Sister Clevora said with a wink.

"You could always apply to be an Embervyne Ranger," Maek suggested, trying to dig himself out of the hole that he'd fallen into face-first, "their leader is a woman, and they get to travel the land."

"They only get to scout for Beckonthrone, it's forbidden to engage in actual combat," Vyra said with a scowl, "I want to charge into battle aside my brothers and sisters. I want to actually be involved."

"The front line is a dangerous place to be," Maek said, shaking his head.

"Not as dangerous as where you'll be if you keep running that mouth of yours!" Sister Clevora snapped.

"Do you rest the entire night, Maek?" Vyra asked calmly.

"Of course, why wouldn't I?" Maek answered.

"I only sleep half the night, the other half I train," Vyra explained.

"Since when?" Maek said.

"Ever since we first came to Brightmeadow Manor," Vyra replied.

"That's a long time," Maek admitted as he scratched the back of his head.

"Vyra, I know what you should do!" Jeuvine added excitedly. "You should make a wish to The Midnight Wolf to become a squire."

Jeuvine was the manor's queen of gossip. If anything stirred up drama, she fully supported it.

"Are you serious? The Midnight Wolf is a mere fable," Maek countered, "a myth. And even if it was true, the tale goes that The Midnight Wolf will only grant a wish if it is for another. The wish cannot be for oneself."

"I'm sure there's a way around it," Jeuvine countered.

"The tale also says that if you try to outsmart the wolf with clever words and trickery, it will emerge from the mist and gobble you up!" Maek said.

"I know I'm right," Jeuvine argued, raising her head, "my friend Sulvina made a wish to The Midnight Wolf asking for bigger breasts.

35

Now when she goes to market, every eye around is staring at her bulging chest."

Vyra glanced back at Maek. The cringing expression on his face revealed his doubt for Jeuvine's story, and he was obviously struggling to figure out a reply to that comment about female breasts. He was failing grandly, giving the women all a good laugh.

Vyra remembered bits of the tale of The Midnight Wolf, mostly from ghost stories shared amongst the orphans in her childhood; each time it was told it seemed like had a new twist to it. Certain pieces had always remained the same: The Midnight Wolf lived in the heart of The Scarred Forest, a land forbidden by the decree of King Sargedon, strangely, as well as any other land that promoted hounds, mythical or not. The Scarred Forest was a dangerous place, full of wild beasts and monsters. Even the Silverclad Knights, led by the great Lord Aldrean, would not venture there. While such avoidance would scare most away from such an adventure, it did not faze Vyra.

This might not be a bad idea, to visit The Midnight Wolf, if it exists, Vyra thought. *If Lord Aldrean's views are humbled, perhaps he would allow me the opportunity to prove my skill, that I would make a good squire and—*

Vyra paused, her facing warming as she remembered her dream from the stables.

"Well Maek *the man*, what do you have to say to *that*?" Jeuvine said, raising her head triumphantly.

"I say that I think I'm going to need some ale after this ridiculous banter," Maek said, sighing deeply and dropping another shirt into the hot water. He turned towards the stairs and all but ran for the door.

"Where are you going?" Sister Clevora yelled after him.

"To get more soapwort from the garden. Maybe I'll visit The Midnight Wolf on the way, ask it to make Jeuvine forget how to speak," Maek replied, flinching as Sister Clevora shot a glare at him.

"Watch out for the forest gremlins," Jeuvine said with a laugh.

~

A soft knock on Maek's chamber door woke him from slumber.

Strange, it's a bit late in the evening for visitors, even for one of Amberleen's surprise performance lectures of how I'm "a sub-par servant," Maek thought wearily as he rose from bed.

"I'll be right there," he said as he slipped into his pants. He quickly weighed the risk of how much trouble he would get in for greeting the visitor without his shirt. If it was Amberleen, it would be extra chores for a week; but laundry day was tomorrow, and all of his shirts were dirty from labor, and Amberleen would drag him through the mud if he greeted her wearing a dirty shirt as well. It really was a no-win situation.

Maek swore his heart skipped a beat when he opened the door to find Vyra standing at his door.

"Hey," she said softly.

"Oh, *hey!*" Maek said, instantly regretting his failure to hide the surprise in his voice.

"Can I come in?" Vyra asked.

"Uh... yeah — sure — *of course*," Maek replied, bumbling over his words. *She still wants to talk to me? Even after I made a bumbling ass of myself earlier?*

"Thanks," Vyra said quickly as she walked by him.

"Hey, I want to apologize for earlier. I know you're the strongest fighter among us servants, and that you can hold your own. I just don't want to see you get hurt. I care about you, Vyra," Maek said, using up every ounce of his courage.

"It's fine, I know you didn't mean ill of me. I care about you too, Maek," Vyra said kindly.

She sounds nervous, Maek thought, well Witch's Blight, I'm also nervous! What is she doing here at this late hour?

"I want to ask something of you," Vyra said, biting her bottom lip.

Hammer of the Titans! What could she possibly want from me, this late in the night? Nobody is up this late, unless they want — wait...

could she really want — with me? Maek thought, a wave of excitement, followed by anxiety sweeping over him.

Maek silently cursed himself for not having a clean shirt to wear when he opened the door. Maek's muscles were toned from the hard labor, but his body had always leaned towards being skinny instead of carved, bulky muscles; it had always been that way no matter how hard he pushed himself, an unwanted birthright.

Maybe it's better I'm not wearing a shirt? Maek thought, wishing for the thousandth time that he had more experience in these matters.

"Sure, what do you need?" Maek replied, putting every ounce of effort he could into sounding composed. His words came out sounding much more smooth and casual than he felt.

O-o-o-o-o, I sounded confident. I sounded strong, maybe even mysterious. Yeah!

"Alright, here it goes," Vyra said, taking a step towards Maek.

Don't screw this up; just believe in yourself. You know what you're doing Maek. You know what you're doing, Maek thought as he approached Vyra. He looked down into her eyes, she looked up into his. Then, he gently leaned down to kiss her.

"I need your help distracting the guards at the city gates," Vyra said, oblivious to Maek's approach.

"Oh, *that's* what you need," Maek said, quickly veering his head sideways, in a desperate attempt to look like he was just turning.

"Yes, I need to get out beyond the walls, but city women who are not part of the Embervyne Rangers aren't allowed outside the walls at sunset," she continued, utterly oblivious.

"Well, it could be dangerous out there," Maek replied reflexively. "There could goblins roaming the lands." He stepped back and leaned on the edge of the bed.

"Maek, I can take care of myself," Vyra said, squinting with irritation, "I've bested you every time we've sparred with the broomsticks. I'd probably survive out there longer than you could."

So I guess everything wasn't just 'fine.' I guess that also explains why she's dressed like she's ready to go on a journey, Maek thought as

38

he looked Vyra over. He cursed silently again for having spent most of their conversation staring at her lips.

"Yeah, you're right. It's a stupid rule," Maek apologized.

"I'm not worried about the wild; I just need to get past the guards."

"Okay, but where are you going?"

"I'm going to the Scarred Forest."

"Have you drunk too much wine?" Maek said, stumbling backwards in shock. "Apart from the Fallen Mountains, that's the most dangerous place in this realm! King Sargedon has decreed it forbidden! Why would you ever want to visit such a desolate place?"

"I'm going to make a wish to the Midnight Wolf," Vyra explained calmly.

"Now I *know* something is wrong," Maek said, putting his hands on her shoulders. "Vyra, you're one of the strongest people I know—"

"I'm one of the *only* people you know," Vyra said, raising an eyebrow.

"That doesn't matter," Maek countered. "You're quick, agile, clever, and good with a broomstick. But the roads aren't safe to travel at night. You heard about the remains of that caravan found south of Beckonthrone; that was on one of the safer roads! Even if you *do* make it and the tales *are* true, The Midnight Wolf is a demon. Not even Lord Aldrean and the Silverclad Knights have ventured that far."

"If I'm vigilant enough, I bet I could make it," Vyra said stubbornly, her small hands forming fists.

"You'd be seeking death," Maek replied darkly.

"Will you help me or not? I just need your help getting past the guards. I can handle The Scarred Forest by myself."

This is an insane idea, Maek thought, *but it sounds like this means a great deal to her. And she's definitely athletic enough; I don't think she has a weapon, but she could probably outrun a goblin or two if they crossed her path. But if it was something worse...*

"Sister Clevora will have your head for this, and that's only if Amberleen doesn't get you first," Maek said, raising his eyebrows.

39

"I won't get caught," Vyra explained with a smile. "It will be our secret."

'Our,' it sounds so pleasant to the ear, Maek thought.

"You're absolutely crazy," Maek said, and sighed deeply, "but... if you are dead set on this, I rather help you see it through, than caught by the guards and rotting in a dungeon."

"Great! I'll grab a few more items and then we can depart. You're the best, Maek," Vyra said, rushing in to embrace him. She gave him a kiss on the cheek, then dashed out the door.

And you, Vyra, are my muse, Maek thought, touching his cheek where she kissed him. *I just hope I'm not helping in getting you killed.*

The moon had just begun to rise in the night sky as they made their way down the cobblestone road; the lights around the city gates guided their path like a lighthouse beacon through the hazy night.

"This fog is perfect for you sneaking by them," Maek schemed, "I'll act like I just came from a nearby tavern."

"Do you think that will be enough? There's at least four guards at the entrance," Vyra asked.

"Trust me, I am the King of distractions. All eyes will be on me. Just try not to pick their pockets as you pass. Not this time at least," Maek said with a grin.

"It is just like old times, isn't it?" Vyra asked with a warm smile. Maek felt like he would be happy just staring at that smile for the rest of his life.

"It is indeed," he said, returning the smile.

Why wasn't I this calm and collected when we were back in my room? Maek thought. *I guess it wouldn't really have mattered. Her mind was elsewhere anyways.*

"Ready?" Vyra's voice snapped Maek out of his regrets.

"Of course," Maek said, "now get out of here."

"Yes sir," Vyra replied, flashing Maek one more smile before she turned and disappeared into the mist.

"Alright," Maek said to himself as he walked towards the Aeroma city gate, "just like old times."

~

Edmund gripped his spear tightly.

Eygodon's piss, it's cold out tonight, he thought, scratching his short, blond beard.

"Oi, Frankfurt, don' it seem cold as the grave out here?" Edmund shouted to a guard on the other side of the gate.

"What?" Frankfurt yelled back, looking his way. Frankfurt had eyes that looked like they belonged on an old hound dog; he was the oldest stationed at this entrance, though the only way you could really tell was from his attitude.

"Don' it seem cold as the grave?" Edmund shouted again, walking towards the other side of the gateway.

"No," Frankfurt replied indifferently, "and I don' see why it matters. Where's Sam?"

"He's taking a leak," Edmund said.

"Ale runs through that boy like a waterfall," Frankfurt said with a brief chuckle.

"That is does," said Bran, the chubby, bald guard next to Frankfurt.

"Are you cold?" Edmund asked turning to Bran.

"Aye, seems now tha' the mist owl has landed, the frost crow be descend'n soon after," Bran said with a grunt.

"Nah, he jus' getting in yer head now," Frankfurt punched Bran on the shoulder.

"I jus' sayin' it's a tad cold, that's all," Bran protested.

"Ah! Quit yer weeping! Both o' yah!" Frankfurt spat.

"I jus' sayin'. We could start a fire. Keep us all warm, and we could see more o' the dark too," Edmund said, gesturing to the pile of tinder stacked against the city wall.

"Start a fire, you say?" Frankfurt replied, his eyes raised he followed Edmund's gaze to the pile of wood. "With *that* wood?"

"I don' see why not. Plenty to go around," Edmund said with a nod. Bran grunted in approval.

"You mean *that* wood?" Frankfurt repeated, pointing to the same tinder Edmund had pointed at.

"Are you deaf? 'Course *that* wood!" Edmund replied.

"Same wood we're supposed to use to show through this fog to signal to the archers atop the city wall that we're bein' attacked? *That's* the wood you want to use?" Frankfurt said, squinting to emphasize his disapproval.

"Second thought," Bran added, "maybe a fire i'nt such a good idea."

"Uh... well...you know, I jus' thought—" Edmund began.

"Yeah yeah! I know! You always *jus' thinking*!" Frankfurt interrupted. "But you're not supposed to be thinking! You supposed to *be guarding*!"

"Sorry, Frankfurt," Edmund shrugged, "cold must be getting to me head."

"*It's not cold*!" Frankfurt shouted, fuming. "Now get back to yer post before I go find that mist owl, and knock you over the head with it—"

"Hey, someone's coming," Bran pointed at the silhouette staggering towards them.

"Hey! You're not s'posed to be out this late!" Edmund shouted to the silhouette. "It's past curfew!"

"Maybe you should ask 'em if it's cold," Frankfurt said, snickering loudly.

"It *is* cold out," Edmund muttered as the three guards approached the silhouette.

"Oi, you need to go 'ome," Bran shouted.

"Terribly sorry s—sir, just lost me way, that's all," Maek replied through slurred speech.

"Well, you found the city gate, lad," Edmund put his hand on Maek's shoulder, "your home is the other way."

42

"I'm *re-a-a-aally* lost, sir!" Maek grabbed the guard's arm and swirled around, leaning into him, "could you carry me back home?"

"*Witch's Blight*! Get off me!" Edmund shoved Maek away. "Do I look like a horse to you, boy?"

"The world is spinning re-a-a-ally fast. I could be on a horse now!" Maek ran in circles, flapping his hands like a bird, then tripped and stumbled into Frankfurt.

"Control yer'self, boy!" Frankfurt yelled, pushing Maek away. "The stables are by Brightmeadow Manor, 'or the brothel is just down the street, 'pends on the kind of ride yer look'n for."

The guards chuckled. Maek continued to spin around.

"Brothel? Never been to one, what's it li-i-i-ike?" Maek asked, swaying back and forth.

"You really neva been?" Edmund asked, scratching his head.

"I'm not surprised," Frankfurt said with a huff, "boy acts like he's neva felt the touch of a woman."

"Hey, I kno-o-o-w things!" Maek protested as he stumbled over to Frankfurt.

"Sure you do, boy," Frankfurt laughed.

"You hold their face like this and give them a bi-i-i-g smooch!" Maek said, grabbing Frankfurt's head and leaning in to kiss him. Before his lips could meet Frankfurt's, the guard's fist forcefully met Maek's stomach.

Maek gasped and keeled over, then vomited on the ground.

"*Eygodon's piss*, boy! Get a hold of yourself!" Frankfurt shouted, "or you be spending the rest of yer youth in the city dungeon!"

"Hey, did you see that?" Bran asked, motioning behind them.

"See wha'?" Edmund asked.

"Though' I saw somethin' run by," Bran explained.

The guards looked around, Maek continued to gag.

"Maybe Sam finally came back from his new job try'n to build a new lake," Frankfurt said with a laugh.

"No, I really though' I saw—," Bran began.

"I'm *sorry!*" Maek's shout was loud enough that all three guards jumped in surprise, then turned to glare at him.

"I didn't mean to cause no trouble, sirs," Maek continued as he stood back up.

"Well, t'was a bit funny," Edmund said with an annoyed shrug.

"I got no more patience for you, boy!" Frankfurt spat, "now off with you before I decide the only thing yer to be kissing is iron shackles!"

"Seems like an odd one, he could be into that," Bran said with a grunt.

"Shut yer trap, Bran!" Frankfurt barked.

"Yes sir, I'll take my leave now, sir," Maek said. He took a quick bow, then turned back towards the city and disappeared into the mist.

"Well, seems like you knocked the drunk right out've him," Edmund said with an approving nod.

"What can I say, ma' fists are divine," Frankfurt said with a chuckle.

She sure took her bloody time, Maek thought, pulling himself to an upright position and wiping his lips as he walked back towards Brightmeadow Manor, *I was running out of tricks; and that cursed oaf of a guard punched me so hard I lost my dinner, now I have to go to bed sore and hungry.*

It was all worth it if it helps her out though, Maek thought as he turned back towards the gate, now just a blur of light in the dark blue haze of night.

Just please be careful, Vyra.

Chapter 5

$\mathbf{V}$yra slipped through the thigh-high grass of The Cinder Fields. Tall dewy blades dampened her skirt in the night

The commotion at the gate behind her seemed to be dying down.

I hope Maek is okay, Vyra thought, cringing as she recalled the sound of a fist striking Maek in the stomach as she slipped silently passed the guards. She had not dared to pause and look back; every moment being near the gate light and the guards significantly increased her risk of getting caught. *I won't be able to forgive myself if Maek ends up in the dungeon for this.*

Distant lights to her right marked the town of Effelshire: Beckonthrone's close and economically prosperous neighbor. If the guards had noticed her slipping by, they would head there first, presuming to find her in town or along the road. No one would expect her to head towards The Scarred Forest; and even if they had, they would not follow her once she entered.

The moon slowly shifted behind the dark clouds in the sky. A cool breeze flowed across the prairie; Vyra shivered, holding her arms closer as she ran. She knew was prepared, but had she come prepared enough?

Vyra noticed movement in the corner of her eye; she quickly ducked into the tall prairie grass. She concentrated on softening her breathing as her eyes scanned the mist.

Vyra grasped the handle of the iron dagger holstered at her hip. She was not sure how much protection it would truly provide if she encountered more than a goblin or two, but it was all she could afford with her meager savings. Though a goblin would only be slightly taller than the prairie grass, the movement seemed to be coming from higher than that.

Vyra quickly thought through all of the possible creatures she could think of that could be roaming the grassland this late at night. Bandits would be the least of her troubles; she suspected that she could handle one or two without breaking a sweat. Goblins would not be a problem unless there were more than two, or if they were wearing reinforced armor. Faeries, pixies, and other forms of fae didn't usually stray far from their forest homes, so that ruled them out. She quickly pondered the likelihood of being able to outrun a bear or a drake whelp. The worst case scenario was a troll. Trolls came out at night, but generally stuck to streams and rivers, none of which were nearby. There were tales of the occasional wandering troll, sighted roaming lands outside of its predictable habitat. *However, if it is a troll, surely I would have felt the growing thuds of its footsteps, right?*

Another flicker of movement made the hair on the back of her neck stand up. It was in the sky. Dread filled her as she thought of more possibilities. If it was a drake, she might be able to sneak away if it hadn't caught her scent yet. A dragon had not been sighted in these lands; but if it was a dragon, she was already dead, and half the kingdom would probably join her shortly. Gryphons stuck to the coastline, and she had never heard of one in these parts.

Vyra tensed as a dark shadow flew in her direction. The fog grew as it soared closer, until Vyra could not see the stalks of grass directly in front of her. All she could see was the fog, and the shadow gliding

46

above her. The shadow flew on open wings, its darkened body almost blending in with the fog around it. The only contrast was its large, round eyes. The eyes were a shimmered glow, a pool of wonder.

That's... a mist owl, Vyra thought, her worry shifting quickly to awe. She had never seen a mist owl before. The natural elements within the world were often manifested through creatures that were alive yet not actually living. The mist owl for fog, the frost crow for late-season snowfall, there were even stories of a glistening blue butterfly that brought the early-season rainfall. Where ever the mist owl flew, the fog would forever follow. If one was to slay the owl, the ambiance around it would cease, and the fog would lift. This was not something that was easily done, as the mist owl was more a force of nature than a creature. It would take extremely powerful magic to harm a frost crow, if one even dared to do so; it was taboo to try and harm the manifestations of the natural weather.

What a sight to behold, Vyra thought.

She watched the mist owl in reverence as it flew past her. The thickness of the fog thinned as it disappeared from sight. Leaving the safety of her thicket, Vyra continued onward.

The moon was near its apex by the time Vyra passed the first tree of The Scarred Forest. It was not difficult to pinpoint its edge. The trees were unique to the region, their bark appearing to fold in on itself as it swirled upward to twisted, lifeless branches that somehow defied the passing of time. Gnarled and jagged, they gave the forest a haunted and foreboding aura.

Vyra slowed her pace as she stared into the deadwood thicket looming ahead.

I'm close, she thought; trying to suppress the feeling of dread as she stepped into The Scarred Forest, *please don't let me be a fool for trying this*.

Moonlight filtered through the dead canopy. Vyra tensed as she moved. Unlike a natural forest, there was no sound of owls hooting, or frogs croaking, not even the gentle hum of insects. Her delicate footsteps on the dry, course earth sounded akin to boulders crashing down a hillside.

Maybe this wasn't the best idea, Vyra thought, trying to fight the rising panic. Every step she took felt like a deafening crash. If there were any eyes in the forest, they were certainly on her now.

No, you've made it this far. You just need to see it through, Vyra told herself, *besides, if there's nothing in this forest, then there's nothing to worry about... right?*

A low rumbling growl answered her question. Instinctively she drew her dagger and whirled around, prepared to fight an approaching beast. But when she saw what made the noise; she gasped silently, her eyes widened and she almost dropped her dagger.

Rays of filtered moonlight illuminated only the jagged edges of the titan. Even kneeling, it still towered over her; its rocky head covered in darkness, only visible by the dim glow from its tiny violet eyes.

A golem, here, *in these lands?* Vyra thought, her mind racing. *How did it sneak up on me? How is it even* here?

There had not been a golem-sighting in Ancantion since the legends of the first travelers that pioneered here. There was no weapon that Vyra felt confident could slay this creature; even a small army surrounding her would bring little comfort to her odds.

The colossus growled again, and the earth shook.

I have no chance of defeating it, but I could try to flee, Vyra thought, *no doubt the golem is faster than me once it builds speed, but the forest is thick. If I darted through the trees, the golem would have to smash through them. That might just slow it down enough for me to escape.*

Vyra tensed her muscles, preparing to leap backwards. She knew she had only one chance at this. The slightest miscalculation and her grave would be nothing but a human-puddle in the forest.

Before she could move, a robed woman stepped out from behind the titan. Her cloak covered her head, swirls of azure and indigo dotted the robe.

"Who are you?" Vyra asked, her voice so high she practically squeaked.

"I am the guardian of the forest; I watch over these sacred lands and keep them safe from intruders. What business have you here, child?" The woman's voice was a dark, smooth melody, echoing in her mind.

"Please!" Vyra confessed, desperation taking hold, "I am merely a visitor, here to seek the council of The Midnight Wolf, to help me humble the heart of The Great Paladin, Aldrean! I don't mean to trespass, and I will not linger! Please, have mercy!"

The robed woman paused, seeming to consider what she was saying.

"I mean you no harm!" Vyra begged, "nor the forest! I am just a traveler!"

The Golem rumbled again, and Vyra almost fell to the ground.

Standing, that golem could easily wade through the trees. To think I could ever outrun such a monster is a fool's dream, Vyra thought bitterly. *Now I understand why not even the Silverclad Knights would dare venture in this forest.*

"You may pass, just this once. Your Midnight Wolf awaits you in the heart of the forest," the guardian said, gesturing to her right, "seek the clearing, make your request to the mist, and do not be discouraged if it does not immediately answer. Just continue the chant, louder if you must. Eventually, the wolf will show itself, in whatever form it takes."

So, the myth is *real*! Vyra thought excitedly.

"Thank you! Thank you for such mercy!" Vyra said, looking in the direction the Guardian had pointed, "I really appreciate your help, and I promise I will leave immediately after—"

Vyra turned back to see that the Guardian and her pet golem had vanished.

Where did they go? Vyra thought nervously. *I mean, that Golem was* huge, *I'm certain it would have made some noise if it had left. Why did I not hear it?*

Vyra shivered as she looked around.

I shouldn't linger here, she thought and began to jog in the direction the Guardian had motioned.

She had not traveled far before Vyra tensed again, noticing lights softly flickering in the distance. She clasped the dagger handle, but released it when she realized that the lights were wisps.

She remembered Sister Clevora telling stories about wisps when she was a child; the spirits of animals now deceased floated harmlessly at night, in the deepest chasms of nature, clinging to the familiarity of their old home.

The Wisps faded in and out between the twisted trees like ghostly fireflies. Though Vyra had never seen one before, she felt a connection with them, as if she had known them her entire life.

Vyra continued onward, the soft glow of the wisps lighting her way; until she came upon several trees that were symmetrically twisted outward, arching to create a wooden tunnel that opened into a moonlit meadow.

This must be The Forbidden Glade, Vyra thought, looking around as she exited the tunnel. Though there was little that she could see beyond the thick fog that encircled the heart of the forest, The Forbidden Glade itself was clearly visible. It looked nothing like the surrounding landscape, its tranquil meadow a sharp contrast to the surrounding nightmarish webs of deadwood. Vyra would have found it peaceful, had she still not been shaken from the ominous encounter with The Guardian and her golem.

Cautiously, Vyra crossed the glade. There was no sign of The Midnight Wolf.

It would be silly to expect it to be that *easy*, Vyra thought.

Vyra found a flat stone rock in the center of the glade, glistening in the lunar light.

This must be the place, Vyra thought, stepping onto the rock and staring ahead. The twisted trees in front of her were wrapped within the earth-bound clouds. She could see nothing outside of the clearing, and the thought of anything in the forest having a clear view of her made her uneasy.

The Guardian of the Forest let me pass, surely that means I will be okay... right? Vyra thought, trying to reassure herself. She remembered

50

Maek's warning: that the wish could not be about herself, or the wolf would emerge from the mist and gobble her up. But what wish would make Aldrean notice her value as a candidate for knighthood? Vyra frowned, Aldrean's encounter with the snotty noble woman from the garden still weighed heavily in her mind.

No time to brood upon that, Vyra thought. *I don't know how long I'm safe in this meadow, if I'm even safe at all.*

She gathered her strength, straightened her back, and began.

"Great Midnight Wolf, please hear my prayer," Vyra shouted into the moon-touched mist.

She paused for a moment; hoping for some sort of response, but also bracing herself for a beast to emerge from the mist and attack her. The only noise was a soft breeze

"Oh great Midnight Wolf, please hear my prayer," Vyra yelled, "there is a great man who is dear to me, but his eyes are not open. Please, help me humble his mind, so he can see potential beyond what is controlled by rules or tradition, and so he may gaze upon others with his heart."

Vyra stared into the murky tree-line. Her hand gently glided over the handle to her dagger as she listened for both a celestial response and an approaching beast.

Not hearing the response of either, Vyra remembered the words of the Guardian of the Forest.

She hinted that it might take time, but how much time? Vyra wondered. Clearing her throat, she began again.

~

Inside a cabin hidden in the twisted trees, Eygodon was pouring himself some wine when he heard Vyra's voice.

"Brielle, was that you?" Eygodon asked.

Eygodon's companion, a tiny nymph glided around the corner. She was almost small enough to be mistaken for a faerie, though her

51

appearance was very different from those wispy creatures. Brielle's naked body was clothed only by the flurry of leaves that continuously flowed about her. With a slender face and a curvaceous body, Eygodon had no doubt she would be heavily desired by many in the fae-realm; but why she chose to stick around *him* was a mystery. Nymphs were only a third of the size of a human, which made little difference to Brielle, whose snarky personality towered above that of most humans when she wanted it to.

"Wasn't me," Brielle said indifferently. She shook her head, her wavy brown hair flowing around the two tiny wooden antlers protruding from the front of her head.

"Perhaps we have a visitor," she added.

"Perhaps so indeed," Eygodon quickly raised his eyebrows as he took a deep gulp of his wine. Setting the glass on the carved, wooden table, he quietly opened the tree house door and stepped to the overhang outside. Brielle floated gracefully behind him.

"Who is that?" Brielle said softly.

Eygodon stared though the fog at the woman in the glade. Eygodon's cabin was nestled in a large tree, several rows back from the clearing. The cabin would likely be shrouded from where she stood, but he could see her clearly.

"I have no idea. Never seen her before," Eygodon replied. Goblin eyesight was actually worse than humans', except in low-light areas like caves and tunnels. However, as half-human, half-goblin, he had the benefits of both human and goblin vision; allowing him to see clearly through darkness and fog, with the only downside being that it was difficult for him to perceive color shades of blue and yellow. In his dichromatic world, greens were shades of bright blue, and actual blue was more turquoise. Every other color was either a bright red or a dull grey. Humans may have found The Scarred Forrest to be a land of terrifying darkness, but to Eygodon, it looked just like the rest of the world.

"Oh great Midnight Wolf...," Vyra began her chant again.

"Looks like another Kae-koon sucker for that *ridiculous* Midnight Wolf myth, come to our doorstep," Brielle said with a shrug.

Kae-koon referenced a human of unmixed blood. Specifically, Kae-koon was fae slang for "nomad," because in their eyes the humans never truly belonged in whichever lands they chose to settle. *Kae-koon's wisdom* was a popular curse word in fae, meaning to believe or do something incredibly stupid. Even Eygodon frequently used that one.

While the human race was one of the youngest races, it had also grown quickly and invasively. The Kae-koon's clashing with the pre-established borders of the elves, dwarves, and gnomes led to cohabitation. However other races were not as welcoming of the invasion. The goblins, fae, and ancient ones such as dragons and sphinxes resented the forced change of their traditional boundaries. The unyielding Kae-koon expansion, combined with the resentment of changing boundaries, set the stage for the great wars.

"Should I summon a beast to send her running back to her pampered life in the Kae-koon town? You know, I bet a snarling boar would scare her so much she'd wet herself. Or perhaps, maybe a badger? Yes, that would give her nightmares *for weeks*!" Brielle asked, her excitement growing.

"She doesn't appear to live a pampered life," Eygodon said, "she looks like a mere servant."

"Kae-koons are all the same," Brielle said with a snort, "piggish, fleshy creatures of weakness."

"Oh great Midnight Wolf...," Vyra repeated.

"Didn't you bed a human once?" Eygodon tilted his head towards the nymph with an amused expression.

"Oh, don't you even go there!" Brielle protested, her cheeks turning pink, "I had drunk a lot of honey!"

"I wouldn't call a teaspoon a lot, even for a nymph," Eygodon squinted at her as he scratched his beard.

"Besides, it's not like we really could do a lot! Don't pretend you don't know what I mean!" Brielle argued, her cheeks reddening by the second.

"No, I don't know," Eygodon said, his eyebrows rising. "Please *do* elaborate."

"I'm not even half the size of a Kae-koon. Figure it out," Brielle said, squinting at him.

"I couldn't tell. From your attitude, I thought you were a giant," Eygodon teased, flashing a wild grin.

"Keep this up, and I will turn you into a fern," Brielle threatened with narrowed eyes.

"The other plants would appreciate my company better than you do," Eygodon replied, pretending to be indifferent with a shrug.

"Oh great Midnight Wolf..."

"Well, we could always talk about *your* previous encounters of the heart," Brielle raised an eyebrow.

"I think I'd rather be a fern," Eygodon groaned.

"I can help with that," Brielle said, cracking her knuckles gleefully.

"I have no doubt you would," Eygodon chuckled softly, "you have the body of a nymph, but the spirit of a dragon."

"*What* — no! That is not a compliment! Those beings are horrible creatures!" Brielle raised her voice. "Rending villages to ash and devouring everything in sight. Why would you compare me to such a vicious creature?"

"*Sssh*! Lower your voice. I only meant that you are a force to be reckoned with," Eygodon explained, "it was meant as a compliment."

"Hmph!" Brielle said, holding her head high and straightening her shoulders. "Well, at least you didn't compare me to a fire sprite. Damn nasty creatures, the gremlins of the sky. I would have hexed you out of this tree for such a comparison."

"If I were to call you that, I would have jumped first and shouted it on my way down," Eygodon said with a grin.

"And I would have conjured up a comfy pile of boulders to catch your fall at the bottom," Brielle replied stiffly.

"Oh great Midnight Wolf, please hear my prayer," Vyra repeated into the mist for the fifth time, "there is a great man who is dear to me, but his eyes are not open. Please, help me humble his mind, so he can see potential beyond what is controlled by rules or tradition, and so he may gaze upon others with his heart."

"I can't believe she's still trying," Brielle said, peering down at the woman below, "I haven't decided yet whether I find it impressive or pathetic."

"A bit of both, really," Eygodon replied with a shrug.

She is quite a pretty flower. How did she make it out this far? Eygodon pondered, finally shifting his focus to Vyra. *She is young, but it is a miracle she is not already wedded to another. A woman that attractive, even if a peasant, should not have much trouble in at least winning the mind and lust of a lesser noble.*

"So... the summon, are we doing this?" Brielle asked, wiggling her shoulders, "because no one would *ever* believe her if it was a pixie-potamus."

"Isn't that just... a really fat pixie?" Eygodon asked.

"Oh no," Brielle said, a wild, mischievous smile crossed her face. "A swarm of tiny winged hippos with spiked hair... *oh*, I'll make it happen."

"Let's hear her wish out first," Eygodon said.

"Really?" Brielle replied, looking disappointed.

"Oh great Midnight Wolf...," Vyra sighed heavily, she sounded almost defeated.

She's really serious about this? Eygodon thought, scratching his chin, *very well...a quick play of moonlight and echoes will do the trick in convincing her to leave.*

The warlock pulled a half-dead leaf from a jagged branch adjacent to his cabin. After chanting a few phrases, he crushed the leaf in his left hand. Grains of light fell from between his fingers, floating into the fog below.

Vyra was about to turn and leave when a flicker of light in the mist caught her attention. Moments later, a wolf bathed in silver light emerged from this mist.

Vyra gasped. She instinctively reached for her dagger, but then hesitated.

"Are you the Great Midnight Wolf?" she asked cautiously.

"That is the name your kind calls me," the wolf replied.

"Yeah, if the ancient runes were written in goblin dung," Brielle said, laughing so hard she almost fell out of the tree.

"*Hush*," Eygodon scolded the nymph, and then focused back on the illusion.

"Are you not already wedded to another?" the wolf asked. "It is not my place to merely satisfy the wishes of lustful desires."

Vyra paused. *Of course not! I've wanted to be a knight since I was a child. But these newfound feelings for Lord Aldrean, what about those? Is my desire for Aldrean purely lustful? No, it can't be. I've admired him long before these feelings grew within me. Sure, there is yearning, but there must be more than that as well.*

"No, I am not wedded to another," Vyra replied confidently, "my dreams until now have only been to be a Knight serving the Silverclad Knights. I have desired nothing else until now."

A woman Knight? Eygodon's eyes widened. *She's really serious? Well, perhaps there might be more to this woman than seemed at first glance. Her ambitions certainly explain why she is not wed or with child.*

"And who is the one whose heart you wish to capture?" the wolf asked.

"It's... the Great Paladin, Aldrean. I serve in his manor, and admire his discipline. But I am not of noble blood, so he hardly notices me, either as a warrior or a woman," Vyra said solemnly.

Eygodon clenched his fist so hard it drew blood.

Aldrean!   That worthless scoundrel wrapped in fancy armor, Eygodon thought, fuming, *you have such high aspirations, Vyra, yet your standards for love barely rise above dirt. Primal desires, I could at least understand, but desires based on status alone...*

"Yuck. I'd rather bed a bog sprite," Brielle spat.

The wolf only stared at Vyra. She tensed.

"Have I done something wrong? Is that too much to ask?" Vyra asked nervously.

Wait! Perhaps I can use this opportunity to finally strike at Aldrean, Eygodon thought, *she did say she was close to him, after all. I could use that to my advantage.*

"I will consider your request, but first I have one to make of you," the wolf replied.

"Anything, what do you ask?"

"Move aside! I'm taking over!" Brielle said, her eyes glowing green as she darted in front of Eygodon.

"Remove your clothes," Brielle said, and the wolf echoed.

"Remove my — *what*? Excuse me?" Vyra asked, a look of shock and bewilderment on her face.

Brielle snickered. Eygodon stared at the nymph in shock.

"You commandeered my illusion, and you're having her do *what*?" Eygodon asked, open-mouthed.

"If she wants to be another scratch on Aldrean's bedpost, she'll have to endure my trials first," Brielle said with a mischievous grin. "Besides, you were just going to request she assassinate Aldrean for you."

"I was not!" Eygodon protested, "I had an elaborate plan, a full intrigue, scandal, and—how'd you know that was my plan?"

"It's okay," Brielle continued to stare at Vyra, but patted his shoulder, "I still think you're pretty clever for a half Kae-koon."

"Thanks," Eygodon replied flatly.

57

"What importance does that have to my wish?" Vyra asked, squinting at the wolf.

"O-o-o-o-o-h, good question," Brielle turned to Eygodon with a smirk, "she's figuring you out, *Great Midnight Wolf.*"

"*You're* the one telling her to take her clothes off!" Eygodon countered.

"You're actually complaining that I took your boring plan and made it more interesting?" Brielle asked, raising an eyebrow.

"I'm all about raining down molten fire upon Beckonthrone," Eygodon explained, "but I am not just going to make her strip naked in the forest!"

"So there's something *wrong* with being naked?" Brielle asked, gesturing quickly to herself with a huff.

"You know that's not what I meant," Eygodon replied. "I just prefer to be a respectful sorcerer."

"Warlock," Brielle added.

"Sorcerer," Eygodon corrected. "Give me control of the illusion back."

"Certainly," Brielle replied, her eyes glowing brighter, "right after this."

"Well?" Vyra's eyes narrowed.

"I am a merely a spirit of the forest," the wolf replied. "We are servants to nature itself. It is the sacred way to only make deals with those who are not afraid to show their natural form in the presence of the uh — creator of life."

"I guess that makes sense," Vyra said, considering what the wolf had said, "very well, then. If that is how it must be."

"Here, you can have your illusion back… I'm done with it now," Brielle said, the glow vanished, but her eyes were still mischievous.

"Why'd you say *that*?" Eygodon exclaimed, his jaw dropping even further. "None of it is even true!"

"Yeah, pulled it straight from out of my behind! I can't believe she actually bought that!" Brielle said, covering her mouth to muffle her laugh.

"Last time I include you in on my schemes," Eygodon grumbled.

"You'll come around, you need as many allies as you can get if you're going to ever overthrow the kingdom," Brielle said with a shrug. "Besides, the Kae-koon fixation on clothing is a disease in itself. I'm doing her a favor by setting her free."

"Shove it," Eygodon hissed at the nymph.

There's nothing weird about taking my clothes off in the forest, Vyra thought, trying to reassure herself, *I mean... it's just the spirits of nature.*

Vyra slowly loosened her corset, followed by her dress; her clothing fell to her feet.

Turning back from arguing with the nymph, Eygodon felt the air leave his lungs as he gazed upon Vyra's naked body. He had seen many unclothed in the past, yet this was different. The curves in her plump breasts flowed to a petite waist and down to a ripe round bottom. He felt like he was gazing upon a natural wonder.

"Hey... Eygodon, you okay?" Brielle said, looking at him with concern.

"I — I'm fine. I'm fine. Just trying to decide what to do to her next," Eygodon bluffed, feigning composure.

"Well, she looks pretty cold now," Brielle said, peering down at her.

"I could tell her to put her clothes back on," Eygodon said through shortened breaths.

"And have The Midnight Wolf contradict itself immediately after she stripped naked?" Brielle questioned. "Yeah, that will *definitely* raise suspicion to how realistic this illusion is. Good luck convincing her to make a deal with you after that."

"Elementals aren't supposed to falter," Eygodon cursed. "You've really turned this situation into a pile of orc dung, nymph."

"I could summon a flock of cloth-eating wombats," Brielle replied cheerfully. "Send her running back to town naked—"

"I'm going to gather the herbs for her potion. See if I can clean up the mess you made," Eygodon growled.

"I'm here if you need me!" Brielle said with a wink.

"You've done enough, thanks," Eygodon said sarcastically as he rose and moved towards the edge of the wooden overhang.

Vyra grabbed her arms, trying not to shiver from how cold it felt without the protection of clothing.

"We will form a pact," the wolf replied, "I will grant your wish, but I may ask a favor of you in the future. You must agree you will grant my request, when it is asked of you in the future, no matter what it is."

Vyra pondered the terms. An open-ended request is dangerous. *As it stands right now, I have little to lose. So, there is not much that could be asked of me that could make me worse off than I am now. None of the myths ever involved the wolf asking one to kill another, so it's unlikely that will be his request. It's a risk, but so are many things.*

"I agree," Vyra said quickly, "so long as the request is not that I harm another or myself."

A clever addition, well there goes any possibility of her slaying Aldrean for me. But that still leaves a lot of room for creativity, she must be desperate. Either way, if I cannot harm Aldrean through the request, perhaps I can reach him by other means. It sounds like she earnestly desires this, Eygodon thought bitterly. *Poor child, wanting such admirable heights, yet lusting over such scum.*

"Very well, stand as you are. My acolyte will bring you what you require shortly," the wolf said, howling once before it disappeared into the mist.

"Alright," Vyra replied.

"Nice howl, it was overdramatic but convincing. Now what *are* you doing?" Brielle asked as she moved towards the warlock, but Eygodon had already leapt from the tree house. He landed quietly on the forest floor and stealthily maneuvering through the mist, gathering herbs and mushrooms for the potion he was going to concoct.

It took longer to gather the materials than he had expected, but not because he had forgotten what to gather. He knew the recipe of the potion and thousands of others by heart, but he found himself glancing at Vyra frequently as he worked.

Eygodon paused, noticing a silvery blue mushroom growing against a twisted tree.

Aldrean is a lucky man to have such a beauty desiring his attention, Eygodon thought, grabbing the blue mushroom, *and he is equally as unlucky that she sought aid from me to do it*!

Having gathered all the ingredients, he pulled a mortar and pestle from his robe, followed by a bottle.

I could store an entire apothecary of materials in this magical robe, he thought proudly. *A talented sorcerer is always prepared.*

"Are you... almost done?" Vyra's voice reached through the fog.

"*Patience!*" Eygodon's voice echoed across the glade as the voice of the Midnight Wolf.

"I'm sorry, I'm sorry!" Vyra said, holding herself tightly, unable to stop the shivering. "It's just getting pretty cold out here."

"I'm working as fast as I can," Eygodon muttered to himself as he ground up all of the materials, except for the blue mushroom. He tilted the mortar so the mashed materials fell into the bottle. Pulling a vial of water from his robe, he added the liquid to the mix. He gently waved the bottle in a circle, until the liquid in the potion turned a vibrant violet.

"So... Aldrean," Eygodon whispered, staring at the blue mushroom as he held it over the violet potion, "the Great Sorcerer Eygodon sends his regards. Let's see how untouchable you *really* are."

Whispering an ancient incantation under his breath, Eygodon crushed the mushroom in his hands, and flickers of shimmering white fell from his fingers and into the elixir. The warlock shook the ampoule until the sparkles swirled around in it like starlight.

"Perfect."

Vyra stared into the mist as the moments dragged on.

Did the Midnight Wolf leave? she thought. *Did I do something wrong? I followed the Guardian of the Forest's instructions...*

A silhouette emerged from the mist, drawing closer.

Something is coming. Wait, someone *is coming. A person...a man! And I'm still* naked! Adrenaline flushed through Vyra as she pulled her clothes up from the ground to try and hide her body.

"You have nothing to fear," the robed man said as he approached, "I am but merely an acolyte of the Midnight Wolf."

"Okay," Vyra replied, rushing to dress herself. Vyra could barely see his face over the shroud of his hood. From the little she could see, he appeared quite handsome. She could have sworn she heard a sigh of disappointment from the robed man as she finished dressing herself.

"Here." The man held up a vial of liquid and sparkling light.

"It's — it's beautiful," Vyra stared at it in wonder; but as she reached for it, the man pulled back.

"Your end of the deal." The man reached into his robe and pulled out a glowing red gem, attached to a silver necklace.

"Of course," Vyra replied. "What do you need from me?"

The man twisted the gem and it opened up like a locket.

"A drop of your blood will seal the pact," he said. A white flower quickly grew up from the ground between them. The flower was gorgeous, but its stalk was covered with sharp thorns.

"A drop of blood? That sounds like dark magic," Vyra said cautiously, taking a step back.

"A common misunderstanding of Kae — *humans* with the ancient ways; the routes of what is feared and what is evil may seem similar to the untrained eye, though their results are vastly different," the man explained.

Hesitantly, Vyra knelt to the flower and extended her right hand. She pricked her finger against a thorn, winced, then stood and held her finger over the gem. Several drops of blood fell into its glistening surface, and the man quickly closed the amulet.

Vyra felt a tingling burn on the bottom of her right hand. She turned her hand to see a symbol marked in the palm of her hand. It was only about the size of a coin, and looked like a crescent moon combined with the scratch mark of a beast.

"I'm marked?" Vyra said with concern, "but I heard marks were a result of dark magic, binding someone to—"

"A common misunderstanding," the acolyte interrupted hastily, "again, the natural ways is known only by a few; and what is unknown is often feared."

"I guess that makes sense," Vyra replied, uncertain. "Will it ever fade?"

"When The Midnight Wolf has determined its needs fulfilled, then shall it fade completely. Now your deal with The Midnight Wolf has been sealed," the acolyte said, holding out the vial, "add this to whatever drink your desired will consume, and he will see you in a whole new light."

"I like the sound of that," Vyra said, grasping the elixir.

"May it bring to fruition your deepest desire," the man said. Once their hands touched, the man held onto the potion for a second longer than Vyra expected.

"Thank you, and please thank the Midnight Wolf and the Guardian of the Forest for their gracious aid," Vyra said, flashing the acolyte a warm smile. Then she turned and raced out of the glade in the direction towards Beckonthrone.

"What have you done?" Brielle asked angrily as she floated down next to the acolyte, "you actually *helped* her!"

"Did I though?" Eygodon said with a grin, staring in the direction that Vyra had left. She would probably reach the gates of Beckonthrone within the hour at the pace she was running, though deep down he wished she would have stayed longer.

"I don't know, *did you though*?" Brielle asked mockingly.

"I got what I wanted, and even more," Eygodon said, holding up the shining red amulet. Brielle's eyes widened as she looked at it.

"She thought it was merely a binding spell. That Kae-koon must know *nothing* of magic! She would have had a better bargain if she had just given you her soul," Brielle said, shaking her head with disbelief. "So, what are you going to do with all that power that she just handed you?"

"Currently, nothing," Eygodon said, tucking the amulet back in his robe. "The true gift was what I gave her."

"Well, what was in that potion you gave her?" Brielle asked, her eyes wide with mischievous curiosity.

Eygodon looked in the direction of Beckonthrone.

"Exactly what I told her," he said with a grin.

"Being cryptic and mysterious is only sexy to Kae-koons," the nymph said flatly, "the rest of us just find it obnoxious."

"Just keep any beasts off her until she gets out of The Scarred Forest. It's a miracle she got this far unscathed," Eygodon said, shaking his head. "Maybe put a Distraction Jinx on the guards at the gate entrance too. They *really* wouldn't want to confiscate that elixir."

"Fine, but you're telling me everything when I get back," the nymph replied as she straightened her shoulders and glided away.

"Fair enough," Eygodon said, looking down at the traces of shining blue residue still in his hand, "I can hardly wait for it myself."

Eygodon blew on his hand, sending shimmering sparkles across the glade. He started back towards his cabin, but then paused.

What Guardian of the Forest?

Chapter 6

Vyra's bed creaked loudly as she sat on it. Her room was small, with the only furniture being a heavily-aged bed and a worn table; though as a servant she was lucky to even have that much.

Vyra stared at the bottle that she had placed on the table, the bottle that the acolyte of the Midnight Wolf had given her. She did not need a lantern in the room, the sparkling from the bottle cast shimmering lights dancing across the room.

On her way back, it occurred to her that she had not developed a plan for getting back inside Beckonthrone. Vyra almost felt like she had divine favor when she returned to see the guards all leaving the entrance simultaneously to take a leak. She was easily able to slip back into the city unnoticed.

It's so pretty — shit! *How am I going to get him to drink this?* Vyra thought. With a deep sigh she looked at the mark on her hand. She had tried to scrub it off, but the mark from The Midnight Wolf was as attached to her as her skin. *I definitely paid a price for it, but how great will that price be?*

A sharp knock on her door jolted Vyra to her senses. She dashed to the table, quickly wrapping the bottle in a piece of cloth that she often used as a scarf when the frost crow visited. Then she tucked it under the table and went to the door.

Please don't let it be Lady Amberleen, Vyra thought anxiously. The higher ups occasionally performed random room inspections of the servants, to ensure that there was no contraband being snuck into Brightmeadow Manor. Wine, mead, and ale would just be a slap on the wrist; it would be the Umbra-Trade drugs that they would be after.

Centaur Meat was a popular commodity among Umbra Poachers; chewing on even a sliver of centaur meat for even a few moments would provide a caffeine rush to the chewer, even longer would give a huge temporary boost of strength and stamina. It was decreed illegal by King Sargedon, as hunting centaurs would violate the treaty of peace they had with the nomadic race.

A scale from a Mermaid, if added to a drink, served as a powerful aphrodisiac. Mermaids rarely ventured to the shores of Ancantion, so it was an exotic and rare drug. However it was rumored to be more commonly used in the southern realms, especially amongst noble scandals and secret gatherings specifically for deviant sexual ventures.

Pixie Dust was the most dangerous and difficult to acquire. The northern fae hated humans for encroaching on their wild territories, so getting a pixie to sell some of its dust was a challenge only a few well-connected humans had managed. Actually capturing a pixie was nigh unheard of. Using the drug was even riskier than acquiring it. If snorted, it could cause hallucinations so vivid you could touch and feel them; a good trip could give the user an erotic night with the person of their dreams; a bad trip could have their body ripped apart by an abomination from their nightmares, which only they could see. While the dangers frightened many from ever even fantasizing about trying the drug, Pixie Dust was perceived as the pinnacle of hallucinogenic adventures for passionate risk-takers.

While all of these drugs were way too expensive for a servant's budget, the higher ups checked anyways to insure a servant was not making additional coin storing contraband goods for Umbra Dealers.

The higher ups also probably did it as a power gesture of their superiority.

Still, Vyra thought, *if Amberleen or one of her agents found the elixir, it would likely be confiscated and used against me as grounds for expulsion from the manor.*

There was another knock on the door, harder this time.

Vyra held her breath and opened the door.

She let out a sigh of relief when she saw Maek eagerly awaiting her in the hallway.

"So, how did it go?" Maek asked. "I see you're unharmed and—"

"*Shh!*" Vyra hissed. "Come in!"

Maek quickly slipped into the room.

"I'm sorry I wasn't able to distract the guards on your way back. I'm pretty sure if they saw me a second time, I would have wound up in the dungeons," Maek explained.

"What you did was plenty. Thank you so much," Vyra said with a smile.

"So...what happened? You were gone for a while I think. Did you actually go into The Scarred Forest? Did you encounter any goblins?"

"I saw many things!" Vyra said, her eyes lighting up, "While crossing the fields to the forest, a mist owl flew right over me!"

"You *saw* a mist owl?" Maek asked, his mouth hanging open. "What an amazing sight!"

"Then after I entered The Scarred Forest, I met the Guardian of the Forest and her pet golem."

"Pet... golem? But there hasn't been one of those in these lands since—" Maek asked, his eyes widening. He put his hand against the wall to steady himself.

"Since the first settlers of Ancantion, I know right?" Vyra said excitedly, "I thought it was going to kill me, but she let me past... to go visit The Midnight Wolf!"

"Wait," Maek said, tilting his head to the side, "so you saw The Midnight Wolf?"

"Even better! I got to speak with it, and it let me make my wish!" Vyra said.

"*Really?*" Maek said, as his eyebrow rose. "This is a fascinating tale, Vyra. But you don't have to entertain me with stories if you just decided it was too dangerous and turned back."

"*What?* Why don't you believe me?" Vyra protested.

"I believed you at the mist owl, but then the Guardian, *then* the golem, and *then* The Midnight Wolf?" Maek said skeptically, putting his hands in his pockets, "it just seems like a bridge to the unreal."

"Fine, if you won't believe me... then believe *this*!" Vyra said with a glare, she turned, knelt down, and pulled the small bundle of cloth from under the desk.

"*Witch's Blight*!" Maek's eyes widened and he stepped back as the cloth fell from the elixir. "That's filled with magic, real magic!"

"I told you I wasn't just making up *stories*," Vyra gloated.

"Okay, I'm sorry. I believe you," Maek said as he braced himself against the side of her bed. "It's just... a lot to take in."

"I know," Vyra replied, setting the elixir back on the counter. "I wouldn't have believed it myself had I not witnessed it with my own eyes."

"Vyra...," Maek said, taking a deep breath as he looked at the potion. "I'm not a mage, but I've read enough books in the Brightmeadow Manor library to know that there is incredibly powerful magic in that bottle."

"Yeah...the fact that it's lighting up the entire room was hinting to that," Vyra said with sass, "and when did you get to read books in the library?"

"Amberleen and her goons cannot be watching me *all* the time," Maek said with a wink. "So, are you sure you're going to give it to him?"

"I've come this far," Vyra said, looking back at the glistening elixir. "And if it gets me to become a squire, it'll be worth it!"

"How are you going to get Aldrean to even think of drinking that?" Maek asked, raising his hands to his head, "it's sparkling like a damn lighthouse!"

"I'll figure something out," Vyra replied confidently.

"I just hope you know what you're doing," Maek said cautiously, "because I sure don't."

~

Aldrean was sitting against the stone edge of the balcony when he heard a loud pounding against his chamber door. He chose not rise and open it, knowing he had left it unlocked. The paladin continued to stare out at the slowly brightening sky as he heard the clanking of armor moving in his direction.

"It's almost dawn," Orbit said as he stepped out onto the overhang. "Orbit is surprised to actually find you in your room alone!"

"Sometimes I wish my balcony had a trap-door. I think pushing you through it would decimate more invaders than a boulder or hot oil," Aldrean said with a snarl.

"That would be a poor move," Orbit replied, "Orbit would get a head start in killing more enemies than you. Then King Sargedon would appoint Orbit as the new Paladin of Beckonthrone and Orbit would get this luxury chamber."

"You would not want to be Paladin, Orbit," Aldrean said softly.

"Orbit would not mind giving it a try," Orbit replied, straightening his shoulders. "The mass of ladies that you herd to your room would alone be plenty a reward."

"Yes… two-faced noble women who only seek to bed you because of your status. What a reward *that* is," Aldrean replied with a sigh.

"If it is so much a problem, than why not pursue the affection of someone beneath the noble class?" Orbit asked, raising an eyebrow.

"I am the Paladin of Beckonthrone, the leader of the Silverclad Knights. With the goblin attacks becoming more frequent, worry and

70

concern spread through our kingdom like wildfire. I am the idol the people turn to when they seek safety and reassurance. Because of this, I must appear flawless, pristine, and unreachable."

"Orbit does not know many who think you are pristine," Orbit added.

"You're missing my point," Aldrean said, shaking his head. "The noble class of Beckonthrone has a grasp on this kingdom; they've convinced the people to believe they are superior to them, that they are stronger than them, and rightfully deserve to be treated as such. As the face of Beckonthrone's might, I must only make actions that embolden that strength. Pursuing the affection of someone outside of the noble class would show the public that I am human just like them, with all the flaws and weaknesses that each human has; their confidence in Beckonthrone would slip, and our internal peace would be no more."

"Are these your words, or the words of our King?" Orbit asked inquisitively.

"The words of King Sargedon," Aldrean confirmed.

"The situation is more complex than Orbit had expected," Orbit said with a huff.

"The King has a good heart, but being a cat has made him a bit of a bastard," Aldrean said.

"As true with many cats," Orbit added, cracking his neck. "Perhaps he would be a kinder king if we just gave him some warm milk?"

They both chuckled for a moment.

"He almost died in the Battle of Cinder Reign. If the Duskpetal Witch had succeeded... and even after..."

"Yes, it was a close call. Too close for Orbit's liking," Orbit added.

"The King was the strongest warrior of us all," Aldrean said. "I'm not sure if he had ever even considered defeat or death before Cinder Reign. Since that day... he has not been the same. I am not talking about his appearance, his mind has changed too. Only a select few know the king is actually a cat; I feel that the whole kingdom knows that something has changed with his leadership. Trying to maintain the normalcy is an additional weight that I carry."

"Orbit does not know the solution to our cat king's problems," Orbit said, "but Orbit does know the solution to yours."

"Oh, yeah? And what's that?"

"Make Orbit the new Paladin. Orbit would invite *plenty* of normal folk up to this chamber, and the kingdom already knows Orbit is perfect."

"Not a chance, Orbit. As the Paladin, I cannot falter and I cannot walk away… not until the warlock Eygodon has been slain."

"At least with our recent victory, no further travelers will meet the wretched fate of those that perished with that caravan south of Beckonthrone," Orbit added optimistically.

"I hope so," Aldrean replied with an uncertain tone. "Nevertheless, my duty continues."

"Very well," Orbit turned and walked towards the door. "Then Orbit will continue to outperform you until the king fixes your problem by appointing Orbit as the new Paladin."

~

Vyra was running chores when Orbit the Omnipotent's loud voice reached her ears. She turned to see the overly armored gnome talking to Amberleen at the manor entrance.

"Ah, Orbit cannot wait for the banquet tonight! Orbit will feast until he requires the blacksmith to forge him a larger breastplate!" Orbit said with a laugh. "Do you perhaps, have a sample of the meal that Orbit can test in the mean time?"

Why is he always wearing his armor? And why does he always refer to himself as if he were another person? Vyra thought.

"I am sorry, milord," Amberleen apologized, "but we only have so many to prepare the meal. I am afraid it will not be ready until this evening."

This — this could be my opportunity to get close to Aldrean! Vyra thought. *Orbit might actually be useful here.*

72

"Oh Great Orbit, it would be an honor if I could help," Vyra said as she rushed over, stretching her face to look exceptionally eager.

Amberleen gasped, scowling as she whirled around to face Vyra.

"You speak out of place! It is not the place of a servant as low as you to assist in the matters of serving the nobles' food. That duty falls to the maids of the manor," Amberleen lectured.

"Nonsense," Orbit interjected, patting his armor, "all are equal in the admiration of Orbit the Omnipotent."

"But Lord Orbit, it is not the way things are done," Amberleen said in anxious protest.

"Make an exception this time," Orbit replied with a loud chuckle, "Orbit likes this little-one's spirit. She has fine taste in those she worships."

Funny who he is calling "little," I'm at least twice his height, but I might actually be able to pull this off, Vyra thought excitedly.

"You flatter me, oh great Orbit," Vyra said with a bow.

"Keep up that attitude, it will get you far!" Orbit said, beaming at the attention.

Amberleen opened her mouth to argue, but Orbit motioned for her silence. The Head Housekeeper fumed as Orbit stepped towards Vyra; reaching into his pocket, he pulled out a small, red-taped vial and handed it to Vyra. She made sure to grab it with her left hand, so no one would see the mark on her right.

"Thank you, milord!" Vyra said, straining to put as much interest into her voice as possible. "But what is it?"

"It is an elixir from the apothecary, said to provide a minor boost to one's overall well-being, providing a resurgence of strength and endurance."

Wow, great, even I could afford to acquire a potion this basic with my budget, Vyra thought flatly.

"Wow! Thank you!" Vyra shouted.

"Orbit gives these out to all his admirers," the gnome said, beaming as he pointed at the vial. "The real gift is on the back."

73

Vyra turned the vial around to see Orbit's signature scribbled on the back.

It's an... autograph, Vyra thought, it took significant mental strength to restrain herself from rolling her eyes.

"You honor me with such a gift!" Vyra yelled, almost squeaking from the additional effort to sound excited.

"Think nothing of it," Orbit said, holding his arm up to pat her on the shoulder. She knelt so he could do so.

"But milord, you cannot be serious—!" Amberleen protested.

"It is decided," Orbit said, turning to leave. "Orbit better see her there."

Vyra smiled as the gnome walked away, each step a loud clank from all his armor.

Anxiety rippled through Vyra as she turned her head to find Amberleen's inches from hers.

"You think you're so clever, chumming up to the noble-class in hopes that it will help you climb the ladder. Make no mistake, child. You are nothing but a servant-girl, and as long as I am the Head Housekeeper of Brightmeadow Manor, a servant-girl is what you shall remain."

"Which you might not be for much longer, if Orbit doesn't see me at the banquet," Vyra daringly shot back.

"You act above your station and think too highly of yourself. You were nothing but street-scum when you came here," Amberleen hissed. "He probably won't even remember a face as forgettable as yours."

"Are you willing to take that risk?" Vyra challenged. Moments passed as she stared defiantly into Amberleen's glare. Then Amberleen's mouth twisted into her regular fake smile and she pulled back.

"Fine, you can have your moment in the sun," Amberleen said with false civility, "bet you won't even know what you're doing. Make one mistake and you're gone, from the banquet, and from this manor."

"I've seen the preparations before, I know what to do," Vyra said.

"You better, because I'll be watching. One mistake and you're back to that gutter you climbed out of," Amberleen turned and walked away.

It'll be worth it, for tonight, Vyra thought.

~

By the second knock on Vyra's door, she had already dashed across the room and grabbed the elixir. She had feared this would happen, but also was prepared for it.

That rotten Amberleen isn't going to sabotage my plans with a surprise room inspection tonight, Vyra thought, quietly opening a loose floorboard and tucking the elixir underneath. Vyra moved so quickly that she was at the door by the eighth knock.

She opened the door, prepared to stare down Amberleen's scowl, but instead met Sister Clevora's worried expression.

"We need to talk," Sister Clevora said sternly.

"Of course, anything for you, Sister," Vyra said, forcing her voice to sound oblivious.

Sister Clevora entered. As Vyra shut the door, Sister Clevora quickly looked around the room, and then turned to face her, her eyes narrowed.

"Heard you started a mighty feud with Lady Amberleen, and that you're going to be serving the Silverclad Knights in the dining hall," Sister   Clevora   said.

"You are correct, Orbit granted me the opportunity. He is rather fond of me," Vyra boasted.

"Orbit is fond of his own reflection, and anything that pretends to be it," Sister Clevora said flatly. "What are you up to?"

I want to tell you, Sister, Vyra thought, *I want to tell you everything. But I've come so far, I can't risk this failing now. The less people that know, the safer everyone will be.*

"What do you mean?" Vyra replied, feigning innocence.

"What's in your hand then?" Sister Clevora asked, staring at her right arm.

Vyra looked down, realizing that she had tightened her hand into a fist to hide the mark from The Midnight Wolf. To Sister Clevora's sharp eye, it must have only come off as more suspicious.

"Nothing," Vyra said quickly. "You worry needlessly. I merely want to perform my duties."

"Oh, I'll have none of that," Sister Clevora said with a frustrated tone. "I was not born a fool, nor did I raise either you or Maek to be dull witted. I know you are a bright and clever girl; wouldn't have been able to steal half the coin you did as a child had you not been gifted. But don't think I'll fall for your trickery. I am no fool, Vyra, and I'm insulted that you would treat me as such."

"Your accusations are in vain. I'm just trying to work my way up the ladder, like you always wanted. To seize an opportunity and gain favor with the nobles," Vyra smiled defensively, letting irritation shroud her guilt for lying.

"Is that how it's going to be then?" Sister Clevora said, her look of anger shifted to sadness. "I don't know what you're scheming, Vyra. But please, be careful. You're playing with dangerous strings if you're trying to puppeteer the noble class. You could lose more than just your station here. Anger one of them enough, and you could lose your head."

"Well, it's a good thing I'm just serving them food then," Vyra replied, almost convincing herself of her own lie.

Sister Clevora rested a hand on Vyra's shoulder as she moved towards the door.

"I hope whatever you're chasing after is worth it, dear," Sister Clevora said. Then she walked out of the room, shutting the door behind her.

I'm sorry, Sister… but I have *to do this*, Vyra thought. Staring at the shut door, several tears slid down her cheeks. *Great changes never come without great risk.*

She took a deep breath.

And this is going to be the greatest of risks.

Chapter 7

The enormous dining hall of Brightmeadow Manor was already extravagantly decorated by the time Vyra arrived. Silver, gold, and cobalt ribbons, the colors of the Silverclad knights, decorated the exquisite walls. The tablemats were already covering the long tables, and the silverware and plates had already been set.

Amberleen must be having the maids work overtime to ensure I have as little involvement with this as possible, Vyra thought, her hand gliding across her pocket, the Midnight Wolf's potion stored safely inside it. *That's fine with me; I only need to do one thing tonight.*

Vyra had used Orbit's cheap endurance potion to water the soil, then carefully refilled it with the elixir. The taped sides would muffle the glimmering of the potion, and no one would question why she had a potion with Orbit's signature on it; they were a common item among anyone who he suspected was an admirer.

Lady Amberleen stood watch adjacent to the wall near the center of the hall, overseeing the festivities like the statue of a gargoyle in fancily dressed clothing. One cold glare directed in Vyra's direction made her shrink. It sent a clear message that she would do nothing without Amberleen's approval.

Many of the guests were just taking their seats as Vyra entered the dining hall to refill their drinks. King Sargedon sat at the very end of the long table, still adorned in his full-plate armor that lent an almost foreboding presence about him. None of the other knights were wearing their armor, except for Orbit.

"Impressive that you arrived before all of us!" one of the knights shouted, only quickly glancing at King Sargedon before looking back to his plate. Most of the knights seemed too intimidated to even dare look in the King's direction, which may have been intended.

"I care deeply for all of my subjects, and make a point of arriving early and being the last to leave," King Sargedon replied confidently. The King had already been sitting in the largest chair at the end of the table, decorated in his royal armor.

"All hail King Sargedon!" Lord Aldrean shouted out.

"All hail the King!" the knights shouted in unison, and then took their seats.

"So speak, how did it go?" Ethoria, the tall red-haired woman in leather armor asked through gulps of ale. Ethoria was the head of the Embervyne Rangers, the scout and reconnaissance division of King Sargedon's forces, and the only guild that a woman was permitted be a part of. While there were rumors that the Embervyne Rangers saw occasional combat, officially they had not been allowed to fight since The Battle of Cinder Reign. Vyra suspected Ethoria sought combat as much as she did. Though Vyra wanted to be more than a Ranger, she had a deep admiration for her nonetheless.

"We wiped those vile creatures from the land!" Orbit shouted gleefully. He slammed his goblet against the table, ale splattering over the edges. "They should have known better than to trifle with *Orbi-i-i-i-it the Omnipotent*! Well, they've learned to fear Orbit *now*!"

"Yes, you plowed into them faster than a rogue barrel rolling down a hill," Aldrean said flatly.

"And still a more impressive feat than some of the things that you've plowed into!" Orbit shouted with a smirk.

"Majesty," Aldrean said sternly, lowering his head to his interlaced hands that were resting on the table. "I request you permit me to test the sturdiness of Orbit's armor by allowing me to use him as ammunition for one of our catapults."

"Control yourselves, both of you! This is a time to celebrate, not quibble over who wields the biggest sword," boomed King Sargedon's voice, though his body did not move a muscle. De'eyzen, Sargedon's royal advisor, stood so closely next to him it almost looked like he was holding him up.

Vyra had not seen King Sargedon except in the royal parades, and only when she was a child. From what she remembered, he was as titan of a human, with arms the width of oak trunks, and the ground rumbled as he walked. Some had said that he was the son of a titan; others said he was the descendant of a God. She had been looking forward to seeing him in person. While Vyra had expected it from Orbit, she was perplexed as to why King Sargedon was wearing full-plate armor at the dining hall; even his face was covered. And why did it sound like his voice was coming from his stomach?

A maid whispered something in Amberleen's ear, and she reluctantly turned and exited the area.

This is my chance, Vyra thought.

Vyra eyed a tray of goblets in the corner of the hall. Making her way to the side of the room, she put her hand over a goblet as she poured the elixir into it. Mixing it with ale dulled the glimmering lights until it was no longer visible.

I hope it's still potent enough to work, she thought, careful to keep track of which goblet had the potion in it as she walked across the dining hall.

"*Agreed*! Besides, if we were competing over who is the bravest, we all know it would be *me*," Ethoria said with a smirk.

"That is why we keep the rangers from the front lines," Aldrean said comfortingly. "You are our secret weapon."

80

"Shameless flattery," Ethoria said with a slight smile. "It would be nice to see the real battle— "

"I will not risk all my forces being in one place, not after Cinder Reign," King Sargedon said.

"But it was *because* we arrived that—" Ethoria began.

"This is not a subject we will be discussing again," King Sargedon replied sharply.

"But our rangers are skilled fighters. You *know* this! They have proven to be just as useful on the battlefield as—" Ethoria began.

"*Enough!*" King Sargedon snapped.

Ethoria leaned back in her seat, silent but frustrated.

"So," King Sargedon continued, "do we know if the Duskpetal Witch was behind the goblin attack?"

"Hard to say, your Majesty," Aldrean said.

"And why is that?" Sargedon asked. "What did they say?"

"*EEEEAAAAHHHHHH!!! RAAARRRGGHHH!!!*" Orbit shouted.

Vyra jumped, almost dropping the drinks from the surprise.

"*Witch's Blight!* What is wrong with you, Orbit?" Sargedon bellowed.

"That is what they said, but Orbit does not speak goblin," Orbit replied with a shrug.

"None of us do, and their leader was slain before we could capture and interrogate him thanks to… Orbit," Aldrean said, casting a glare at Orbit.

"Orbit did not know he was the leader! Orbit does not speak goblin!" Orbit protested.

"He was the only goblin actually wearing a robe. You would have noticed that if you looked his way with your eyes *before* your hammer," Aldrean groaned.

"He could have been a mage. Orbit had to act before he had cast a nasty curse upon us. Orbit had no idea, and could not ask because *Orbit does not speak goblin!*" Orbit yelled.

"Did he have a spell book, a wand, or a staff?" Aldrean asked, rubbing his temples. "Only the most powerful mages can cast spells without the aid of a tool."

"Oh, ah, well then… he did not," Orbit said, scratching his beard. "Upon further consideration, Orbit believes he might have been the leader."

"And the only one who could have likely spoken both our tongue and goblin," Aldrean concluded.

"Okay, well… how many were there, at least?" King Sargedon questioned.

"Only several dozen, your Majesty," Aldrean said. "We were able to slay them without any—are you going to pour that or just stand there watching us?"

Vyra jolted to attention as she noticed Aldrean staring up at her. Orbit, Ethoria, and King Sargedon followed his gaze.

They've noticed me! Think of something to say, fast!

"Well?" he said, raising an eyebrow.

"I'm terribly sorry, milord! You seemed in an important conversation, and I was waiting for its completion as I did not want to interrupt!" Vyra said.

"Ah!" Orbit recognizes you!" Orbit pointed and her and grinned, "go easy on her, Slayer of the Sheets! She is new and not normally accustomed to these duties."

"Your humor grows old, Orbit," Aldrean said, flashing Orbit a glare but then turning back to Vyra.

"I did not know you were new to your duties. Please, accept my humble apology," Aldrean said, his voice a smooth melody.

"Think nothing of it, Lord Aldrean," Vyra said, trying not to blush as she refilled their goblets, but handed Aldrean the goblet with the potion mixed into the liquid.

Please… let this work, Vyra thought.

"Why does *he* get a new cup?" Orbit asked, squinting at Aldrean, "Orbit is the one that invited you to the privilege of working in the hall."

Witch's Blight! I'll never see beyond a dungeon wall for the rest of my life, Vyra thought, cringing internally.

"Please forgive me!" Vyra said to Orbit. "This was a new blend of wine that Head Housekeeper Amberleen requested specific approval of Lord Aldrean. I will happily bring you some if he approves it first."

Aldrean stared down at goblet warily.

"You said you're new to this position?" Aldrean asked. There was a tone of caution in his voice. He set the goblet down and stared into the liquid as if he was studying it.

Eygodon's piss! Does he suspect it's poison? Vyra cursed. *I had not planned for this!*

"Yes — yes milord," Vyra said, stumbling on her words, "We just needed your approval—

"Oh *really?*" Orbit asked, and then leaned over the table, reaching for the goblet, "Orbit *loves* a new drink! Orbit will try it first!"

"Keep your grubby lips off!" Aldrean snapped, pulling the goblet out of Orbit's reach. "I will not share your spit."

"Orbit does not see why not. You share everyone else's spit," Orbit grumbled as he sat back in his chair.

"As this woman has so earnestly said, Amberleen has requested I be the one specifically to try this," Aldrean said with his head high. "And I will see her request fulfilled."

Vyra inhaled deeply as Aldrean lifted the goblet to his lips and tasted the liquid.

"It is, well, it is… um," Aldrean began.

Vyra forgot how to breathe.

"Quite delicious, actually," Aldrean said, and downed the rest of the goblet, "please tell Head Housekeeper Amberleen that I approve of her creation."

I can't believe this actually *worked!* Vyra thought, beaming.

"Immediately, milord," Vyra said with a wide smile. She quickly turned, starting for the exit.

"Wait!" Aldrean shouted. His voice sounded stern.

Vyra froze; she could have sworn her heart skipped a beat.

She slowly turned around to face the Paladin. He had an inquisitive look upon his face.

"Yes, Lord Aldrean?" she asked, trying to hide how nervous she felt.

"What was your name?" Aldrean asked.

"It's Vyra, milord," she replied.

"It's a pretty name," Aldrean said with a warm smile, "well, thank you for the opportunity to try that delicious drink, Vyra. You may go now."

"It was my pleasure," Vyra smiled and walked quickly down the hall.

Could it have taken effect so quickly? Vyra thought. *No, he was just being kind.*

Vyra's feeling of triumph was quickly erased by Amberleen's rigid voice.

"Well, since you're still *here*. We might as well make use of you," the Head Housekeeper said with a growl. "The main course is about ready. See it served to our knights with haste, or this is the last time you'll ever see the inside of the manor's walls."

"Right away, milady," Vyra said obediently.

I need to play along, at least for a while, Vyra thought. *I won't be able to talk to Aldrean about being a squire if Amberleen sees me removed from the manor grounds before the elixir even kicks in.*

Fortunately Vyra did not have to wait long. She had just finished helping serve dinner when she heard Aldrean's voice over the dinner commotion.

"Please, excuse me," Aldrean said, standing up from the table and making a hasty retreat from the hall. It looked like he was heading towards one of the Brightmeadow Manor towers, towards his room.

"Hmm. It seems that Lord Aldrean no longer has the fortitude for holding his ale. Orbit has surpassed him in this, as he will in other things soon enough!" Orbit said with a hearty laugh.

It looks like the potion might be taking effect! Vyra thought excitedly. *This might be my chance to ask him. I could finally become a squire!*

Vyra's hopes faded when she locked eyes with an approaching Amberleen.

"Your efforts were overwhelmingly a disappointment," Amberleen lectured, her mouth curling to a sinister grin, "the food is served quickly and without hesitation. Not only did you fail to do that, you disrupted the serving process by bringing your dishes to the wrong location. You, child, have *failed*."

"That's not possible! I had the location for each dish memorized!" Vyra protested. She had watched each platter delivered many times in the past, she knew their designated locations by heart.

"Perhaps for a normal meal, your presumptions would have barely met par. But this was a ceremonious occasion. There were specific instructions on where to place each dish, which were given at the gathering earlier today," Amberleen scoffed.

"Specific instructions — you never told me about a special gathering," Vyra said, her fists clenching as she stared at the Head Housekeeper.

"You said you could handle this, my dear. It's not *my fault* you overestimated your capabilities," Amberleen said snidely. "Now I want your things gathered, and you out of Brightmeadow Manor by sunset, or I will personally see to it that your new lodgings are the city dungeons."

Vyra could almost feel Amberleen's triumphant smirk as she pushed past the Head Housekeeper, gently sobbing as she ran out of the hall, and down the passage way that led to the higher levels of the manor.

Once out of sight of Amberleen, Vyra immediately stopped crying.

It's all or nothing now, she thought, *hopefully this will work!*

She made her way up the winding stairs and down ornate hallways that made the bare small wooden passageway to her room feel like a dungeon. She was almost out of breath by the time she finally reached the exquisite wooden doors leading to Aldrean's chamber.

Vyra knocked gently on the door.

"Who is it?" the voice was definitely Aldrean's, but he sounded agitated.

I should ask permission to enter, Vyra thought. *Eygodon's Piss to protocol, I'm out of here regardless!*

Vyra gently opened the door. She had never seen Aldrean's chamber before. It was easily twenty times the size of her small room. The walls were covered in banners, elaborate designs, and hand-painted portraits of battles. His bed was as wide as Sunpiercer's horse stall, and covered in lavish silk sheets. Beside the bed was Aldrean's sword: a long spotless blade ran to its guard, a cyclone of swirling metal, frozen in time. Metal thread entwined the rest of the grip, ending in a fancy metal pommel. Above the bed was a large marble bust of a man, with a symbol on its forehead that Vyra did not recognize.

Aldrean sat at the foot of the bed, his head in his hands.

"May I enter?" Vyra asked, trying to project some form of politeness.

"As you wish," Alrean replied, sounding distant.

"Is everything okay, milord? You left in quite the rush," Vyra said, moving closer to the bed.

"I do not feel my usual self," Aldrean replied, shaking his head.

"I know the feeling," Vyra said, the realization of how far she had gone to pursue becoming a knight hitting her all at once.

I've gone too far, I risked my life, almost had Maek thrown in the dungeon, I've lost my place at Brightmeadow Manor, and now I've drugged one of the most noble knights in all Ancantion. I just wanted a chance at proving myself, to become a knight. But at what cost? Is this all worth it?

Aldrean groaned and shook his head.

I might as well go pack my bag before Amberleen summons the city guards, Vyra thought.

"I'm sorry," Vyra said, and then she turned to leave.

"Sorry for what?" Aldrean asked.

Sorry for giving you that elixir. That was cruel of me, Vyra thought.

"I'm sorry for bothering you," Vyra said, "I'll take my leave now."

"No," Aldrean said, his head still in his hands.

"No?" Vyra repeated with confusion.

"I mean, please… stay," Aldrean said, his voice calmer now.

"What for?" Vyra asked.

"You came here for a reason; I would like to hear it," Aldrean said.

Is this it? Is this my chance?

"Lord Aldrean, I have no greater desire than to help protect the kingdom. I have trained physically and mentally in to become a swordsman, and in hopes of one day becoming a member of the Silverclad Knights."

"Is that so?" Aldrean asked, rubbing his temples.

"If you would just give me the chance, milord; I would wish to prove to you that I could make a capable squire."

Aldrean shook his head again, and then looked at Vyra through squinted eyes.

"Uh, ye—yes… I will take you on to be a knight," Aldrean said, looking somewhat dazed.

"That's amazing! Thank you milord! I will prove my worth! I won't let you down!" Vyra shouted with joy.

Aldrean's eyes widened as he looked at her.

"What's wrong?" Vyra asked with concern.

"But you're a — a woman, and you're…"

"I'm what?" Vyra asked, growing impatient, "I'm fully aware that I'm a woman. But I've trained harder than most for this opportunity! I'm ready, and I'm capable."

"Yes, it's just you're a woman…" Aldrean began, and then swallowed hard.

"It's just that *I'm a woman*?" Vyra yelled, losing her composure. "Tell me, milord, if I can best every other squire in the Silverclad Knights, then why should being a woman hold me back from being your squire? I deserve the right to be able to prove myself! Why won't you grant me that?"

"It sounds like you are quite capable and determined, but..." Aldrean said meekly.

"But *what*?" Vyra asked, still very irritated.

"You're a woman... and you're *actually* talking to me," Aldrean said in disbelief.

"Uh, come again?" Vyra asked, baffled. "Lord Aldrean, plenty of women talk to you."

"They *do*?" Aldrean asked meekly.

Is this some sort of trick? Vyra thought. *Is he toying with me?*

"Very funny, Lord Aldrean, but the whole kingdom knows about you are quite the— er... the *experienced* knight."

"I am?" Aldrean asked, sounding confused. "I'd think I'd recall something like that if it were true."

"Don't play games with me like this, Lord Aldrean," Vyra snarled.

"I'm sorry! Please don't be mad," Lord Aldrean begged.

"Wait a moment," Vyra said, staring into Aldrean's eyes. His expression did not seem to be teasing, or manipulative. In fact, he looked confused, desperate and...genuine?

"What — what's wrong?" Aldrean asked.

Witch's Blight! Vyra thought, her eyes widening, *I think he's actually being sincere*! *What was in that potion I gave him*? Vyra thought.

Chapter 8

"Things are going quite well, wouldn't you say?" Eygodon said as he sat on the window ledge in his cabin. The moon cast a silver hue across his jagged dark hair as he peered through a spyglass of dragon bone; exquisite carvings of runes and scriptures in an ancient language wound across the spyglass. The bones of dragons were one of the hardest substances known. Eygodon did not know whose magic was strong enough to carve into dragon bone, but the spyglass served as a humbling reminder that there was always a bigger, mightier fish in the magical sea.

"Well?" Eygodon asked. He lowered the shining relic to the nymph.

Brielle peered into the spyglass.

"I do not know how she can tolerate Aldrean," she said, pulling her head back. "Even seeing through *her* eyes, he looks pathetic."

Eygodon pulled the spyglass back, taking one more glance into it before popping the red gem out from the end.

"Thank you, milady," Eygodon said, staring at the glowing red amulet. "Looking through your eyes has saved us the inconvenience of having to infiltrate Beckonthrone to see when the spell would take effect."

"Did you have any doubt?" Brielle asked, curious.

"Not the spell, no," Eygodon replied, "but who knew if she'd actually be able to pull it off. I expected a while longer, it's impressive that she was able to give him the potion so quickly, don't you think?"

"I guess," Brielle said with a shrug. She hopped up from the deadwood-carved chair that was way too big for her. "I still don't understand what your plan is, or what exactly your spell did to Aldrean. Every time I ask, you just give me another one of your obnoxious riddles. If I wanted those headaches, I would have joined forces with a sphinx instead of a warlock."

"Sorcerer," Eygodon corrected.

"Whatever," Breelle said, rolling her eyes. "So are you going to tell me or what?"

"Do you remember my fight against the humans during the Battle of Cinder Reign?" Eygodon asked, fiddling with a deadwood twig. His eyes glistened bright amber in the rays of moonlight filtering in through the cabin window.

"Nope. The Fae actually care very little about the petty affairs of Kae-koon," Brielle said. "I'm pretty sure I was stocking up on honey and had the affection of a lovely faerie with a face that could make your body quiver with anticipation."

"Lovely," Eygodon said with a chuckle. "Well, that Battle was the turning point in the great war of this land. King Sargedon led the attack, as usual."

"That was right before you lost your previous love, right?" Brielle asked, showing a bit of interest. "Right before you got chucked like a pebble in a pond!"

"She left me, yes. But let's move on from that," Eygodon grumbled.

"Fine, carry on with your dull story," Brielle mocked, though she leaned closer to listen.

"The humans— the Kae-koon call it the Battle of Cinder Reign, because though it was in the dead of winter, King Sargedon blazed through the blizzard, leaving fire and embers in his wake."

"Is King Sargedon a demigod?" Brielle asked.

"No one knows, though I'm pretty certain he's currently a cat," Eygodon said with a chuckle.

"You see, King Sargedon never lost a battle that he personally led. It was baffling! We had to wage war around his personal guard to gain any ground on him," Eygodon explained. "When we were finally forced to confront his army, The Duskpetal Witch concocted a plan to turn the battle in our favor, and obliterate the king once and for all. Our forces were losing ground when—"

"He stopped the ritual right before it was completed. Yeah! Yeah! I've heard this part already," Brielle interrupted.

"You are no fun to tell stories to," Eygodon said with a groan. "Fine, the ritual activated prematurely—"

"Explains why you got dumped," Brielle interjected with a snicker.

"Will you *actually listen?*" Eygodon growled.

"Will you get to the point? I didn't ask to listen to your memoir," Brielle countered, lying down with her head in her hands.

"Sure. So though the ritual failed to kill the King, it was not completely ineffective. The King, he was enfeebled. With the king reduced to a more vulnerable form, I seized the moment to try and capture him."

"*And?*" Brielle asked, her eyes glued to Eygodon.

"Just as I was about to capture the king, Aldrean swooped in, rescuing the king at the last moment. But it was *just* him; The Silverclad Knights were all but wiped out; my elite goblin vanguard, The Gruharr, had done their job well. Against him alone I would have easily prevailed—"

"Sure you would have," Brielle said sarcastically.

"—but those damn Embervyne Rangers came to his aid. My armies were already thinned, and they made short work of the rest. I was forced to retreat. I lost everything."

"Yes, and *then* you got dumped!" Brielle said with a sharp giggle.

"Of course, *that* is the part you hang onto," Eygodon replied, rolling his eyes.

"What can I say, it is the funniest part of this sad tale," Brielle said, shrugging.

"Yeah, well… the tides seem to be turning in our favor," Eygodon said then briefly chuckled.

"And how is that?" Brielle asked

"Aldrean's strength is in his confidence, diminish that and he's nothing. And there's nothing our little whore of a knight enjoys more than bedding a pretty noble woman."

"But the woman who came to us — the one who wanted help from The Midnight Wolf — I don't recall her name," Brielle said.

"Vyra, her name was Vyra," Eygodon said softly.

"Yeah! Vyra! What good does sending her into his arms help your cause? She wasn't even a noble!" Brielle added.

"Vyra played the most valuable role of my plan. She wanted a potion to humble his heart, and that's exactly what I gave her."

"And here we are with the cryptic messages again," Brielle groaned.

"Let's take a trip to The Whispering Isles. Surely there's got to be at least a few out there still loyal to me. Maybe we can make something exciting out of this new opportunity."

"And what opportunity is that?" Brielle asked impatiently. "What was in the potion that Vyra gave Aldrean?"

"It's a specialized curse, crafted specifically for our dear Paladin," Eygodon said, his eyes flickering brightly with mischief.

"Sounds vicious," Brielle replied, her lips curling into a smile.

"Indeed it is. Now let's be on our way. This is going to get good."

End of Part 1

Thank you for reading!!!

What happens next?

Will Vyra really get to become a squire?

Will she win Lord Alrean's heart?

**What wicked scheme does Eygodon have in store for them
both?**

What will happen to The Embervyne Rangers?

Will King Sargedon remain a cat forever?

How will this all affect the fate of the Kingdom?

Keep reading for a Sneak Peek into the Sequel:
Cinder Reign: The Midnight Flame

Prologue

I'd rather rot in the dungeons of Beckonthrone than be here…

Eygodon leapt gracefully across the obsidian spires protruding from the murky waters of The Whispering Isles. The calmness of the water itself sent an eerie chill down his spine. In any other place where the land met the Casteon Sea, there would be the familiar crashing of water against rock, but here the water was deathly still. The only sound was the faint echo of the hollow voices reaching his ears. The half-goblin pushed them from his mind. The whispers would only lure listeners to an early grave, that much he knew well.

"*Careful, now.* Don't slip!" Brielle, his nymph companion said, almost sounding concerned. Buck naked except for the small cluster of leaves floating around her, the nymph hovered nearby, paying no mind to the chill in the air. "I don't want to find out what lurks in the waters below."

Eygodon reflexively opened his mouth to counter with a snide comment, but decided against it. He could tell she was nervous, and she was right to be. The Whispering Isles were the perfect place for his forces to hide, because they were infamously dangerous. There were countless tales of ships being destroyed: tales of vessels by being run against the jagged obelisks rising from the shadowy sea, of crews being driven to madness by the empty voices relentlessly reaching their ears, just by disappearing into the blackened mists entirely.

During the Forming Ages of the human empire in Ancantion, the name the humans called The Third Realm, an old king grew tired of the mysterious disappearances. He sent an entire battalion of warships to purge The Whispering Isles, and not a single one of them returned. No traces of the ships were ever found, to no one's surprise. No wreckage of a ship remained visible within the isles for long. The myth was that a leviathan of dark depths claimed everything that chose to enter The Whispering Isles, though Eygodon shuddered to imagine what sort of creature that would be.

Eygodon's forces had set up a permanent camp on the northern coast of The Whispering Isles. A wiser traveler would take the long route around the isles to reach the place where his goblin minions had long set up camp. But Eygodon was not just any traveler; he was a powerful sorcerer, one who was bad at being patient.

"I don't understand... if you were just going to use your magic and teleport us here, why not just poof us to their encampment?" Brielle questioned.

"A teleportation spell is not something you can just conjure out of the blue," Eygodon replied defensively, "it takes considerable effort to study. For example: you need to be sure that nothing is standing where your destination is, or it's kahblewie for you both."

"I'm actually impressed you know how to do this," Brielle said, "it seems like pretty complicated magic for a warlock."

"Sorcerer," Eygodon corrected.

"That still doesn't explain why you couldn't have still teleported us *closer* though," Brielle pressed.

"Like I said, nymph," Eygodon growled, "it takes considerable effort, countless calculations, and extensive strategy to—"

"So you don't know where your own army is, do you?" Brielle asked flatly.

Eygodon grumbled a string of curses under his breath.

"Impressive," the nymph added sarcastically, as she gently shifted her brown, wavy hair around the one of antlers protruding from her head.

"I had a general idea of where they were, alright?" Eygodon said defensively.

"General idea meaning the complete opposite side of the bay," Brielle answered. Eygodon did not look at the nymph, but he could swear he sensed her rolling her eyes.

"We're heading to where they are at now, okay?" Eygodon said, filling his voice with confidence.

"You mean, where you *think* they are," Brielle quickly countered.

"Well, they weren't on the southern side of the coast," Eygodon answered sharply, "so conclusively, that only leaves—

Eygodon fell silent then couched down.

"Why'd we stop?" Brielle asked. "Do you doubt that they could be on the northern coast now too?"

"Did you hear that?" Eygodon asked, as quietly as possible.

"Hear what?" Brielle replied, matching his volume. "I'm amazed I can hear you over the incoherent babble coming from the beyond."

Eygodon strained his ears to filter out the whispers.

They waited in silence for several moments, and then Eygodon rose.

"Must have been my imagination," he said, cracking his neck.

"As much as I normally would love to seize the moment to jab you, this place also has me on edge," Brielle said, shivering.

"I appreciate your mercy," he responded.

Eygodon looked out across the murky pool. The surface of the water was as smooth as glass.

My mind is playing tricks on me, Eygodon thought, trying to reassure himself. *The myths cannot be true. This place is nothing more than a dead land.*

For a moment, the sorcerer thought he glimpsed something moving beneath the watery depths; or at least, a part of something. He squinted, hoping the strain on his eyes would separate his imagination from reality, but he saw nothing else.

You're worrying yourself for nothing, he thought, trying to render his mind numb. *No denizen of the depths has ever existed in the Third Realm that could do what the myths say.*

"We should get moving," Brielle softly pleaded. "It is not good for the soul to linger in these lands."

"A wise choice," Eygodon agreed, jumping to the next pinnacle.

The only plausible scenario of reality to these rumors, his mind continued, *would be if it was something that wasn't native to these waters, something that came from very far away, something excessively horrific, something like—*

The sorcerer had no sooner turned to leap towards the next spire, when he heard the sound of softly shifting waters.

Eygodon's eyes stretched wide open.

…we shouldn't have come here, he thought as his body tensed.

"Hey, did you hear—?" Brielle began.

"Follow me. *Don't* stop, *don't* look back," Eygodon hissed. Without hesitation, he leapt to the next spire, then the next. The sound of a small gust of wind told him that Brielle was keeping up.

The two darted across the midnight bay. The hollow whispers seemed to grow louder, matching the sound of the wind against his face as he ran. Beneath that noise, he could hear the growing noise of rippling water.

"We have to go faster, Brielle!" Eygodon yelled. Harnessing his strength, he pushed off the spire he was on as he quickly leapt to the next.

"What are we running from?" she asked.

"You don't want to know," Eygodon replied, pushing forward. "Now, move!"

"I'm going as fast as I can!" Brielle replied, struggling to keep up.

"Well, go faster! Or you won't make it!" Eygodon snapped, landing on the next rocky spike.

"I'm a nymph, not a falling star!" Brielle shot back.

Eygodon listened to the sound of the water below.

"It's gaining on us, you need to speed up!"

"I can't!" Brielle shouted.

"*Kae-koon's fortune!*" Eygodon swore. As he landed on the next spire, he turned around to see Brielle racing to catch up. Eygodon's mouth fell open as he peered behind her. An enormous shadow shifted beneath the water, leaving a deceptively small ripple in the surface above.

How did it find me? he thought, fighting back rising panic.

"I've never seen that look on your face before," Brielle said as she caught up. "*What* is following us, Eygodon?"

He grabbed the nymph as soon as she was within his reach and held her against his chest.

"What are you doing?" Brielle asked. He could hear the growing confusion and fear in her voice.

Eygodon responded by crossing his arms and wrapping them around her. Holding her tight, he turned and pushed off of the spire with all of his strength. The sorcerer soared through the air, clearing several spires before landing gracefully on another rocky protrusion. He repeated the motion again.

"You're a pain in my ass, Brielle," Eygodon hissed as he moved. "But as long as you stick by my side, the only way you're going to die is by my hand. Definitely not by what lurks beneath these waters."

"That was... *almost* comforting," Brielle said sarcastically, but she still hugged him close.

Fear coursed through Eygodon as his goblin ears told him that, despite his acceleration and the gentleness of the water, the creature was still gaining on them. He strained his muscles to increase speed, but it was difficult enough to maintain the momentum.

"Eygodon..." Brielle whispered.

"Don't panic, we're going to make it," Eygodon reassured her, even though he was not certain that his words were true. His muscles were already burning from the strain; he was not sure how long he would hold out at this speed.

"I'm sorry for the way I was… being a pain in your ass," Brielle said softly.

"There's nothing to apologize for," Eygodon said comfortingly as they flew towards the next spire.

"There is… you're being tender and sentimental. I was clearly too soft on you," Brielle said. He could practically hear her smirk.

"I can always throw you back towards our purser. I bet you'd make *fantastic* fishing bait," Eygodon purred.

"There's the Eygodon that'll get us out of this mess," Brielle said, smiling up at him.

Eygodon flashed a quick grin and then looked up. In the distance he could make out the hazy outline of the coast of Ancantion. The gentle roil of the water told him that the creature was almost upon them.

At this pace, we will never reach the shore, Eygodon thought, desperately trying to suppress panic. *I need to make it in the next leap, as impossible as that may seem.*

An earth-shaking bellow swept across the bay, Eygodon almost lost his footing as he landed on the next pillar; his blood ran cold as ice.

"What child of nightmares could make such a noise?" Brielle cried out.

"Stop asking questions! Keep your eyes on me, Brielle. Just promise me that you'll keep your eyes on me!" Eygodon shouted.

He glanced down at Brielle; a terrified expression was etched on her face. Instinctively, she moved to look behind him.

"Don't!" Eygodon yelled, but the sound of his voice was drowned out in another bellow from the beast.

All or nothing, I vowed I wouldn't tap into this power again after Cinder Reign. But against this — I have no choice, Eygodon thought. He quickly positioned himself against an angled slope on the spire. Dark essence swirled around his legs and feet. He pushed forward with all his might; the force so great that it cracked the ground beneath his feet.

Eygodon propelled through the air, flashes of black protrusions merely blurs beneath him. He could see the coast clearly now. The sorcerer hoped that his last bout of strength had been enough.

To his relief, they only seemed to lose momentum as he passed over the shallow water. Eygodon shifted as they fell towards the beach, turning so they would land with his back taking the blow of the impact.

Eygodon clenched his teeth in pain as they hit the sandy beach like a cannonball. Immediately looking down, he felt relief rush over him as he saw Brielle's head nestled against his chest. She had been unharmed by the fall, protected in his arms.

Another blood-curdling bellow brought the sorcerer's attention back to the water. Gently setting her aside, he quickly stood up.

Taking several quick breaths, he clenched his firsts and looked out onto the blackened bay. The spire that he had pushed off of, as well as all of the obsidian pillars he had flown in that final leap over, had vanished. There were no waves from collapsing rock; the water looked completely undisturbed. The only distinction in the flat murky pool was the large shadow beneath the surface.

"Here I am, you bastard!" Eygodon yelled towards the black sea. "Are you here to toy with me, or did you finally come to finish me off?"

The monster bellowed again from beneath the water, the roar gurgled yet still shook the ground.

Eygodon breathed heavily as he watched the darkness move further from the shore and then disappear beneath the murky liquid.

"I can't... I can't believe we actually got away," Eygodon rambled, falling to his knees and wiping sweat from his forehead. "I haven't had an encounter that close since The Battle of Cinder Reign. Hey — I'm sorry about yelling at you back there. You know I wouldn't have done that if it wasn't absolutely necessary, right?"

The nymph remained quiet.

"Look, I apologized okay. Just trust me that it was for a good reason, okay?" Eygodon said.

The nymph did not respond.

"Kae-koon's wisdom, you're a stubborn little creature," Eygodon said with a large groan. "Fine! I'll tell you. But prepare yourself; you're going to be having nightmares for weeks for this."

An eerie silence fell over the beach, without even a tide to break the quiet.

"Brielle, are you okay?" Eygodon asked with concern, reaching towards her.

Eygodon gently rolled her to face him, and then drew a quick breath.

Brielle's face was twisted into a look of terror. Her mouth was frozen mid-scream; the irises of her eyes were a hollow white.

A ground-shaking roar echoed across the beach, followed by soft sobbing.

Hours later, Eygodon awoke, his face against the black sand, lying next to his old friend. He didn't look at her; he couldn't look at her, at least not yet.

"Brielle…" he whispered softly. He dug his hand into the dark sand and watched the grains trickle down his fingers.

"I don't know if — if I can bring you back, my friend. I only know of one way, and even that — even of that I'm uncertain."

A soft breeze blew over the darkened shore. The first sound he had heard since they reached it.

Eygodon clenched his fist on the remaining sand.

"But I'll bring this entire realm to its knees to find out."

Continue the adventure in Part 2 of the Cinder Reign chronicles: The Midnight Flame. Available now at www.vinnwinters.com!

<u>Enjoy Cinder Reign: The Enchanted Elixir?</u>

I'd love to hear about it! Share your experience and help others find it by **<u>leaving a review on Cinder Reign's Amazon page</u>**.
<u>https://www.amazon.com/gp/product/B08XQ5NB8P</u>

<u>Have ideas or suggestions of what you would like to see in the sequels?</u>

You can reach me and keep up to date on current releases at **<u>http://www.vinnwinters.com/</u>**

or at

<u>https://www.instagram.com/vinnwinters/</u>

Thank you again for your time and valuable support
I aim to create more stories for your enjoyment!
The adventure continues!

-Vinn Winter

Want to read more of the Cinder Reign saga for free?

Then join our Readers' Club to receive the exclusive story of Orbit the Omnipotent for free!

Start your adventure at www.vinnwinters.com!

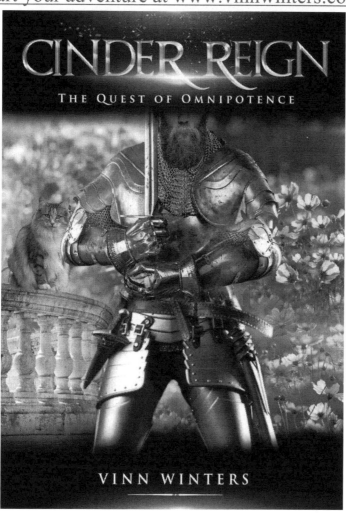

The prequel to Cinder Reign is on Kindle Vella!

More information at www.vinnwinters.com

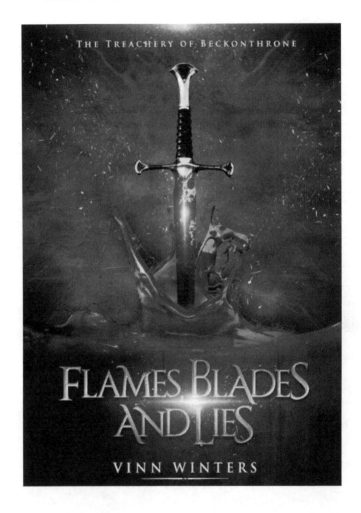

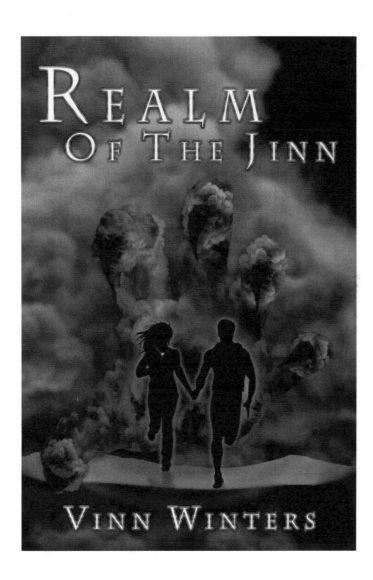

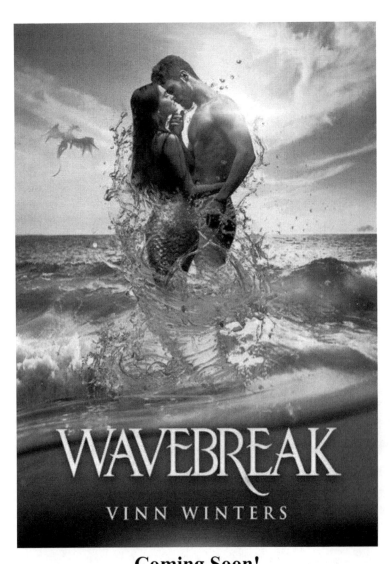

Coming Soon!

Join our Readers' club or follow Vinn Winters on Instagram
to keep up to date on releases!

bout the Author...

om scaling ancient temples, to swimming through Ocean reefs, Vinn
inters loves to chase adventure. When he's not traveling across the
orld, he has two cats that bully him constantly, reminding him that he
obably wouldn't last five minutes in one of his books. He enjoys
laxing over a hot cup of coffee, playing cards, video games, or reading
good story.

Made in the USA
Middletown, DE
12 March 2023

26637674R00068